THE FLESH KING

RICHARD
KADREY

TITAN BOOKS

The Flesh King
Print edition ISBN: 9781835412459
E-book edition ISBN: 9781835412442

Published by Titan Books
A division of Titan Publishing Group Ltd
144 Southwark Street, London SE1 0UP
www.titanbooks.com

First edition: October 2026
10 9 8 7 6 5 4 3 2 1

A CIP catalogue record for this title is available from the British Library.

EU RP (for authorities only)
eucomply OÜ, Pärnu mnt. 139b-14, 11317 Tallinn, Estonia
hello@eucompliancepartner.com, +3375690241

Printed and bound by CPI Group (UK) Ltd, Croydon, CR0 4YY.

Dedicated to David Lynch, a great artist
and a constant source of inspiration

1

It was winter and the weather in New York had turned cold.

Tilda took a strong stance, brought up the Glock and aimed dead center at the target, firing off the six remaining rounds. When the clip was empty, she walked the length of the soundproofed basement to check her results. A smile spread across her face as she took the target down from the sandbags piled against the back wall. Five of the six shots were bullseyes in a tight grouping. The sixth shot hit the target right between the eyes. It pleased her that Ford and Neuland trusted her enough with the gun to let her shoot alone these days. After taking off her ear and eye protection, she hurried upstairs to show them how well she'd done.

The three of them lived in a decommissioned police station near Tompkins Square Park in Alphabet City. The place was a solid three-story concrete tomb set hard into the ground with its barred windows intact. Imposing. Impregnable. They called it the Bunker.

Upstairs, Tilda found Neuland in his lab, which was tucked into the back of the first floor where the cells used to be. He seldom talked about his experiments, so Tilda never asked about them, though she was fascinated by the array of chemicals and potions he had, the stacks of chemistry books and age-stained grimoires.

She walked around his worktable and silently held up the target. Neuland was carefully pouring gray, ground-up raven bones into a flask half filled with a thick yellow liquid, so it took him a moment to notice her. When he did, he removed his goggles and gloves, took the target and held it out at arm's length.

"This is beautiful work. And you've only been shooting a couple of weeks. You're a natural."

She held up her hands and shot finger guns at him. "A natural born killer?"

Neuland chuckled and handed her back the target. "We'll see. Make sure to show that to Ford. He's having a rough day."

"What's wrong?"

"He's calling our old contacts, trying to drum up business, but it's not going well."

"Oh no. I'm sorry."

Neuland leaned on the worktable and said, "He doesn't like us living off your inheritance. Neither do I."

Tilda put a hand on his arm. "But it's okay. I volunteered, remember? I can't fight. I can barely shoot. Hell, I can't even find my way around on the subway. Helping out with money is the one thing I can do right now. And you've both done so much for me."

Neuland pursed his lips. "Thank you. But that target proves you can shoot, so don't sell yourself short. And you'll learn the city soon enough. Ford and I just need to get back on our feet so that this feels like an equal partnership for everyone."

Rolling up the target, Tilda said, "You know, before I met you two no one ever encouraged me to learn things. I mean, not anything that wasn't about my grandfather's business. Nothing for me."

"You'll learn plenty now. Anything and everything you want."

She glanced at his worktable. "Potion stuff too?"

Neuland looked down, thinking. "Maybe. But what I'm working on is dangerous for people like you."

"You mean because I'm alive?"

"Exactly. Revenants like me have a few advantages, and that includes handling certain dangerous chemicals."

"You're locked in here so serious ever since we got back from California. Will you tell me what you're working on?"

"I thought it would be obvious."

"Not to me."

He picked up the flask and held it to the light. "I'm so tired of being dead. I'm trying to find out if I can do something about it."

Tilda smiled at him. "That's wonderful. Will the mixture help?"

Neuland shrugged. "I don't know. I've never tried this approach before. We'll just have to see."

"Let me know if I can help?"

"Of course."

She nodded once and said, "I should let you get back to work."

"Don't forget to show Ford the target."

"I won't."

Tilda leaned up and kissed Neuland on his cold cheek. "Thank you for everything."

"You don't have to keep thanking me. You're one of us now. Part of the team. We do everything we can for each other."

"You have no idea how happy that makes me. I'll really let you get back to work now. Good luck with everything."

Putting on his goggles, Neuland said, "Thanks."

The enormous living room had been the squad center in the old days. Now it was full of comfortable mismatched sofas, easy chairs with reading lights, art from local galleries, and a long conference table where they ate their meals. Tilda loved it. Who would have thought you could turn a police station into something so eccentric and warm?

Ford sat at one end of the conference table looking grim. He held his phone in one hand and pecked at a laptop with the other. When Tilda approached him he eventually looked up and tried to smile, but it came out crooked and wrong.

"Neuland said you were having a hard time, so I wanted to check on you."

"Thanks, T. That's really sweet. I'm just kind of pissed at the world. I'm going through this address book, calling old clients and contacts trying to drum up some business. But no one wants to play." He sat back and ran a hand through his hair. "Maybe coming back to New York was a mistake. Maybe we should have stayed out west and started over."

"No," said Tilda, dropping into one of the conference room chairs. "This is your home. It will work out. You've only been back a couple of weeks. Give it time."

"Maybe," said Ford. "But if things keep up like this, I'm going to have to learn how to ride a scooter so I can start delivering pizzas for five bucks an hour."

Tilda slapped his wrist lightly. "Stop it. You and Neuland are the best at what you do and people know it. They'll come back."

Ford didn't say anything for a while, then nodded to the rolled-up paper in her hand. "What have you got there?"

"A target. Want to see?"

Smiling for real this time he said, "Of course."

As he unrolled it, Neuland came in.

"Damn," said Ford. "That's a nice grouping. What were you using?"

"The Glock G19 you gave me."

"Nice, nice work."

Neuland walked over to the table and said, "Maybe it's time for you to try something with a little more kick."

"Yeah," said Ford. "Maybe a Sig?"

Neuland went to a shoulder holster draped over the back of a chair and brought it back to Tilda. "Tell me what you think."

She snapped the flap that released the gun and held it out at arm's length. It was a lot bulkier and heavier than the Glock. Holding it with both hands, she sighted down the room.

"I like it. A lot," Tilda said.

Ford said, "It's a Sig Sauer P220 .45 caliber."

"It's really heavy."

"True, but the weight helps keep it from snapping back and smacking you in the face. Very embarrassing."

Tilda sighted around the room with it. The gun's bulk made it hard to hold steady at first, but it became easier.

Neuland said, "Some people consider a .45 to be overkill. But in some situations, it's exactly what you want."

"It's what we call a put-down-stay-down gun," said Ford. "You hit someone in the chest with a slug from that and—dead or alive—they're not getting up."

"That's so… cool," Tilda said.

"Want to try it on the range next?" said Neuland.

She grinned and nodded. "Hell yes."

Neuland smiled at her. "We'll try it out tomorrow."

Ford leaned back in his chair and said, "I'm glad we're all in here together, because I want to run something by you."

Neuland sat down and Ford started up again.

"I'm leaving messages all over town and no one's getting back to us. So, I'm thinking we pick out some creep—a real piece of shit—and take him out. No charge. A sort of freebie to reintroduce ourselves to high society."

Neuland scratched his ear. "Who were you thinking of?"

"Benny the Bull?"

"That bastard."

Tilda said, "Who's Benny the Bull?"

Shaking his head, Neuland said. "He does the same work that we do, but he specializes in soft targets."

"Civilians," continued Ford. "Suburban moms and dads who step out of line. Stupid teenyboppers selling hash in the wrong neighborhood. Easy marks who can't fight back."

Tilda sat back on her chair. "That's awful."

"It is," replied Neuland. "Everybody hates Benny. But he's close with his cousin in the Bronson outfit."

Ford raised his eyebrows. "Still?"

"I'm afraid so."

"The pricks. How about that weird little guy everybody calls Igor?"

"The one who talks like Bela Lugosi?"

"That's him. I don't trust him around women or kids. Plus, he's a rat who'll sell you out for bus fare and everybody knows it."

Neuland nodded. "Including the police, and they love him for it. God knows he deserves putting down, but it's probably more trouble than it's worth."

Ford took a sip of the beer that was sitting on a coaster. "Man. It's like you can't assassinate anyone these days."

Tilda raised her hand shyly and both men looked at her.

"You really don't have to do that," said Neuland.

She said, "Okay. But maybe we should do the opposite, and help someone instead of killing someone."

Ford and Neuland glanced at each other, then back at Tilda.

"That's novel," said Ford.

"No one would expect it, that's for sure," Neuland said.

Ford sighed. "But who? We mostly know bastards."

"Really?" said Tilda. "That's kind of sad."

"I guess it kind of is," Ford replied.

Neuland said, "Maybe we need to get out more."

"Definitely," said Tilda. "We should go to a show."

"What kind of show?"

"Broadway! I've never seen a Broadway show."

"What do you want to see?" said Ford.

"*Fly Me to the Moon*. It's a musical of old Frank Sinatra songs. My grandfather was a monster, but the one non-disgusting thing he liked was Frank Sinatra, so I grew up listening to him."

Ford picked up his phone. "I'll get us tickets."

Tilda frowned. "But it's sold out for months."

"I'll get them."

Grabbing his hand, Tilda said, "Please don't assassinate anyone."

"I was thinking more of a scalper."

"We don't kill everyone, you know," said Neuland.

"Yeah," said Ford. "We have strict rules about who we do and don't make dead."

Tilda put her hands on the table. "I'm sorry. I'm still getting used to this life."

"That's okay. There's a learning curve for everyone."

"Thank god," said Tilda and she relaxed a little.

"But you know what I could murder? A rib eye steak. What do you say, T?"

"I'd love that."

They both turned to Neuland.

"How about you? Want to come along?"

"Yes. Please join us," said Tilda.

Neuland shook his head. "Not tonight. I have some work I want to finish in the lab."

"Don't stay in there all night again," said Ford. "You're going to make yourself crazy."

"I won't. There are just some things I want to check."

"Good luck with it." Ford looked at Tilda. "Ready?"

"Yes," she said excitedly. "I can't believe we're going to Broadway."

"We're already halfway there. But don't forget. When you get your coat, bring your gun too."

Tilda stood but stayed by the table. "Do you think I'll need it?"

"Probably not. But you're in our world now and you never know. Can you deal with that?"

"Absolutely."

"I knew you could. Let's hit the bricks."

As Tilda went to get her coat and gun she said, "Goodnight, Neuland. We'll come and check on you when we get back."

"Thank you."

When they were halfway to the door, Ford turned to her. "Maybe we should get Chinese instead."

"No," Tilda said firmly. "I was promised a steak and that's what I want. Thick and bloody."

Ford smiled broadly. "Now you're getting into the spirit of things."

2

There was no night for him. The city was always bright in his ancient eyes.

He sat in that evening's vehicle: an NYPD squad car. The dead cop lay naked on the floor of the backseat and he wore the officer's uniform, easily two sizes too large for his slim frame. Still, all that mattered was the look. The badge. The hat. The belt around his waist heavy with the tools of the police trade. And lastly, the gun. Not that he'd ever used one. All that was necessary was a slight movement of his hand in the direction of the holster and people melted before him. The sight never failed to make him smile. But tonight wasn't the night for games. His body ached with hunger. In truth, he could have sustained himself on the policeman's flesh, but he longed for something softer. Something perfumed. Something perfect.

He spotted the rental car stopped at Seventieth Street off the Henry Hudson Parkway near the river. Certain that the driver was a lost tourist, he activated the lightbar on top of the police car and rolled up behind the rental. Sitting for a moment, he let the red and white strobing lights play across the back window. It was another game. As a policeman, the longer he waited to approach the other car, the more frightened the driver would become. Their fear wasn't necessary, but simply a pleasant addition to what would happen next. After a couple of minutes, he stepped from his vehicle and—even from yards away—he could savor the driver's floral scent. It made his hunger grow.

He took his time walking to the front of the car, letting the driver's aroma grow stronger and richer with each step. When he reached the front door she already had the window down and the smell of her fear mixed with her perfume.

"I'm sorry, officer," she said. "But I'm lost."

He shone his flashlight at her. "May I see your license, ma'am?"

As his prey fumbled with her handbag she said, "My phone ran out of power and I don't know how to work the car's navigation system." When he didn't say anything she added, "I'm sorry," and handed him the license.

He still didn't reply but stared at the small slab of plastic with his practiced police scowl, staying just far enough away from his prey that she wouldn't see the wrinkles that lined his face and hands. She would see them soon, but then it would be too late.

"Your name is Kelly," he said.

"Yes."

"It says here that your eyes are green."

"Yes," the woman replied nervously. "Is that…? I don't understand."

"Green eyes. It's just unusual."

"I suppose. I never really thought about it."

"Of course you did," he said. "When you were a child the other children talked about it, didn't they? They probably called you a leprechaun or something."

The prey didn't say anything for a moment and he could tell

she was caught somewhere between fear and simple annoyance. Eventually, she said, "May I have my license back?"

When he grew bored he handed it to her. The strobing of the lights on the police car bothered her. He watched her try to shield her eyes with one hand, then become self-conscious and lower it. He put a hand on her car door so the prey couldn't roll up the window if she became too frightened. This was the moment when some people would notice his dry, sagging flesh. Much too old for any normal policeman. It was another game he liked to play, but when his prey didn't react he nodded into the distance.

"See that old wreck out there?"

She turned and looked out into the Hudson River at the rusting, metallic hulk of a half-submerged pier. "I do, but I'm already late to meet some friends. Can you just give me a ticket or something and help me get to East Thirty-Fourth Street?"

He took his time replying to the prey. Her scent mixed with the spell of the strobing lights in such a gorgeous way that it made him faint with joy. He knew his hunger was making him weak, but he wasn't ready to succumb to it yet.

He said, "That wreck out there is the Sixty-Ninth Street Transfer Bridge. They built it to move train cars across the river from here in Manhattan to New Jersey."

Quietly, the driver said, "Please, officer. I'd like to go."

He leaned down so that his face was level with his prey's and pointed out into the water. "When they built the bridge, it was beautiful—the light glinting off it at sunrise and sunset."

When she finally spoke, the woman's voice had lost its tone of fear and was now full of anger. "Look, I don't care about any of that. Don't you understand? I just want to go so, please, write me a damn ticket. I'll find my own way downtown."

Still staring out at the half-sunken bridge he replied. "They finished it in 1911. I remember opening day. The mayor gave a speech."

The prey made a face. "What are you talking about?"

He shoved his head in through the car window so she had to lean away and said, "I killed a policeman here that night. Not the first cop I ever killed, just my first New York one."

Even then, the prey hesitated for a second before trying to push him outside, flailing at him with her nails and fists. As she screamed, he clamped a hand over her mouth and said, "It's all right. It will all be over with soon. I hope I get your green eyes."

The prey's hands were wrapped around his wrist, trying to push his hand away. He waited a long moment before relaxing his muscles and letting her shove him. By then, though, even the prey knew it was too late.

The skin of her face and his hand had fused together to become a single thick strand of flesh. Soon, the hands she used to fight him softened, sinking into the meat of his arms as he held her in place. His prey tried one more scream, but nothing came out, as her tongue had melted and flowed into her cheeks, which the policeman slowly drew off her bones and onto his. The wrinkled, pockmarked skin that encased him softened like putty as the prey's new, healthy flesh slid in waves from her body onto his. He felt himself growing strong again and his hunger diminished.

Soon, the prey stopped moving. When he was done feeding, all that was left in the car was a collection of fleshless bones held together by bits of gristle slick with blood and lymph.

Knowing the game had kept him too long where he risked being spotted, he hurried back to the policeman's car and started it. Before pulling back onto the Parkway he couldn't help glancing at himself in the rearview mirror. He had her green eyes all right.

3

At exactly four o'clock in the afternoon, Ford, Neuland, and Tilda's phones buzzed at the same time and with the same message: *LET US IN.*

They gathered around a laptop on a table set against one of the gray concrete walls. The security camera feed from outside showed a group of six well-dressed people scowling up at the lens.

"Shit," said Ford.

"That's troubling," Neuland replied.

Tilda stared at the monitor as Ford said, "T, get your gun but keep it out of sight."

"Who are they? And how did they get my phone number?"

"They're the heads of six of the biggest outfits in town. They have everybody's number."

"Is that normal?" she said tentatively.

"Just be cool. They knocked politely. But if I say shoot—"

"Aim for the middle of the torso."

"Good girl. Whatever this is, we're going to get through it. Okay?"

"Okay," Tilda said.

Neuland pressed the buzzer that opened the steel front door and the gang lords filed in: three men and three women. One of the men was a revenant, as were two of the women. Eddy Jourgensen, one of the living men, and Amanda Goss, one of the revenant women, stepped forward.

"Hi, Ford," said Jourgensen with a faint smile. "How was your vacation out west?"

"Hi, Jourgensen. Same as always. Ate some good food. Killed some stuff."

Goss raised an eyebrow and said, "Hello, Neuland. Still having fun with your chemistry set?"

"Hello, Goss. Yes. Quite a lot of fun, thank you."

"Mama Kelvina says you've come to her for potions," she said.

"Every potion maker goes to Mama Kelvina eventually. No matter how unpleasant it is."

"Watch your mouth," snapped Jourgensen.

"That's right. She's your auntie, isn't she? Lovely woman. Has she poisoned anyone interesting lately?"

Taking a step forward, Jourgensen said, "Shut up, dodo."

Goss shot him a look. "*Dodo?* That's not a nice thing to say to a revenant. Any revenant. So, now it's time for you to watch your mouth."

Jourgensen frowned. "I didn't mean you—"

"Of course, dear," said Goss with a sunny smile. "But don't ever use that word around me again."

Ford cleared his throat. "If you two lovebirds want to bicker, why don't you take it outside?"

Charlie Mendez, another of the living men said, "We're here on something serious."

"Really? We can't get a single one of you on the phone and now you're all here at once. To be polite, what the fuck do you want?"

"We're here to offer you a job," said Goss.

"All of you?"

"Us and more."

"What's the catch?" said Ford.

"You'll be doing it for free," said Jourgensen, looking at Tilda.

"Pass," said Neuland.

"Hard pass," said Ford. "How about you, T?"

She nodded and said, "Pass."

"There it is then," said Neuland. "The door is that way."

Jourgensen held up a finger. "But there is something in it for you."

"What's that?"

"Do the job fast and clean and you'll be welcomed back to New York with open arms. Jobs. Money. Respect. You can be men again and stop leeching off your little Barbie doll over there."

Tilda took a step forward. "They're not leeches. We're a team."

Jourgensen laughed. "Is that what you tell her? A team? You should be ashamed of yourselves."

Crossing his arms, Ford said, "What's the job?"

"Did you hear about the killing last night?" said Goss.

"Which one? This is New York. We're not short on killings."

"The one on the Henry Hudson."

"Nope."

Neuland shook his head and said, "Not a thing."

"I forgot. You're illiterate," said Jourgensen tossing a copy of *The New York Post* on the coffee table. There was a lurid, partially blurred front-page photo of bones on a car seat and the headline *THE SKINNER STRIKES AGAIN.*

Neuland picked up the paper, looked at it, and threw it back on the table. "*The Post.* The gold standard of New York journalism."

"Yeah," Ford said. "For a minute I thought you wanted us to kill the president's alien love child, but this is much more believable."

Jourgensen stabbed a finger at the paper. "Joke all you want, but this prick is raising hell all over town. Which means if cops and reporters keep digging around the story, they just might find that people like us—and you of the dead persuasion—exist and hunt us down for fun. It's hard for any of us to work right now. So, if you idiots can take out the Skinner it gets you back to work. Us too. Everybody's happy."

"Why us?" Neuland said.

"You've done decent work in the past. We thought we'd give you a chance to redeem yourselves."

"Why haven't you done it yourselves?" said Ford angrily. "You've got fucking armies."

Bo Ligotti, a revenant woman, said, "The police are already watching us. But everyone knows you're off the clock."

Jourgensen continued, "The Skinner has been around for a while, but low key. He had a warehouse over in the Bronx where he could take his humps and have all the fun he wanted where no one would find the bodies. They were just missing persons cases. But the wiring was old and the place burned down. Now he's running around the streets with his dick out and a hard-on for the kind of people cops care about."

"Is the warehouse still there?" said Neuland.

"The remains, yeah. At Stony Point, south of Mott Hill."

"Right along the Bronx Kill estuary," said Ligotti.

Ford nodded. "I know the area. I grew up around there."

"How charming," sneered Jourgensen. "Well, get the fuck home and fix this."

Goss spoke quietly, "When the fire department sifted the

ruins, they found bodies—dozens of them—stripped down to the bones, but the cops thought the fire had done it. Now they know different."

"The Skinner isn't stupid. He knows he can't kill in the open forever. He'll be looking for another place to take his toys."

Tilda said, "How do you know the Skinner is a he?"

Jourgensen gave her a look, "'Cause ladies don't do this kind of shit."

"I guess you never heard of Elsbeth Bathory or Joanna Dennehy."

Jourgensen looked around and chuckled. "What are they, some chick band like The Indigo Girls?"

"Yes. Just like The Indigo Girls except Bathory killed more people than you ever dreamed of and Dennehy did it meaner."

Looking annoyed, Jourgensen said, "I can be pretty mean, little girl."

"Look up their names and get back to me."

He turned to Ford and Neuland. "Barbie's got a mouth."

"She's not wrong," said Neuland.

"Maybe. But tell her to watch herself. And you two get to work. We want this cleared up fast."

"We'll need to talk this over," said Ford.

"Sure," Jourgensen said. "You've got one minute."

"And then we kill you all," Goss added.

The three of them went over to the conference table. "What do you think?" Ford said.

"I'm not sure we have any choice," said Neuland. "We can't have the whole city against us."

"Yeah. What do you think, T?"

"I'll do whatever you think is best."

"No. This is group business. We want to hear from you."

Tilda nodded and said, "In that case, I think Neuland is right. We can't fight everybody."

Ford frowned and said, "That's it then." He turned back to the group and said, "We'll do it, but we want back in now. That means when we call, people answer the phone."

"Agreed," said Goss.

"And there's one more thing."

"What's that?"

Neuland pointed to Jourgensen and said, "We want him to apologize to our associate for calling her Barbie. Her name is Tilda."

"And for calling Neuland a dodo," added Tilda.

"First off, Neuland can go fuck himself," Jourgensen said. "As for her, I know exactly who she is. I know how much money she has and I know where's she's from."

Ford said, "Good. Then it should be easy to say her name."

"I don't think I want to."

"Sure, you do. You think we never imagined an ambush like this before? Look up at the sprinkler system."

The six gangsters looked up at the ceiling.

Neuland said, "The pipes are loaded with goofer juice. The stuff that keeps people like me going."

"I know what the fuck goofer juice is," growled Jourgensen.

"Then you know if we open those spigots, it's going to kill you," said Ford.

"And bring you back like me. A dodo."

"What about those of us already on the dead side of the road?" said Goss.

"How many of you are there?" said Ford looking around. "I think with your friends dead we can handle you."

"Do you?" said Ligotti icily.

Jourgensen raised his hands. "All right, stop this shit. I know Ford is dumb enough to try and pull a bluff like this, but Neuland is too smart."

"Thank you," said Neuland.

"But I'm still not apologizing to Barbie."

Neuland took a small cylindrical device from his pocket and held it in front of him. A silver button glittered on top.

"But I will offer you this," Jourgensen said. "The Skinner is a freak for gold. Jewelry. Watches. Teeth. Anything. You pull this off fast and quiet and I'll tell you where it's stashed."

Goss turned to him. "You bastard. You never told us you had it."

"I don't. I just know where it is."

"We're going to have a conversation about this."

"Later," said Jourgensen. "Right now, I want to hear these children say yes."

"So do I," Goss said.

"For gold? Yes. We'll clean up the mess that happened on your watch," said Neuland.

"Fine then. But do it fast. By the end of the week."

"We don't want to see this bastard's face in next Sunday's papers," Jourgensen added.

"Thanks for stopping by," said Ford, gesturing to the door. "You know the way out."

Jourgensen stopped on his way to the door and said, "One week."

"We heard you," Tilda shouted to him.

Neuland hit the buzzer and the front door closed and bolted itself.

Tilda looked at the men. "Do you really have a booby trap like you said?"

Neuland showed her the trigger. It was an antique silver cigarette lighter.

She leaned her back against the wall and laughed. "Thank you. I was so afraid. I didn't want to be turned into—" Tilda froze and looked at Neuland. "Oh god. I'm sorry. I didn't mean—"

"I understand," he said. "I don't want to be like this either."

Tilda put a hand to her forehead. "I think I need to sit down."

She took a few steps and dropped down into a chair by the coffee table. Shaking her head she said, "I didn't mean to start trouble with Jourgensen, but he sounded just like my grandfather. I guess it set me off. I promise I won't do it again."

"Why?" said Neuland. "We thought you were great."

"Really?" She turned to Ford. "You too?"

"Absolutely. You saved us the trouble of punching the prick."

"Oh, thank you."

"You want a drink or anything?"

"No. I think I'll just go to my room and have a nervous breakdown."

"Rest up. It's been a big day."

Standing she said, "So, we're really going to kill the Skinner?"

"That's the plan."

"Are you all right?" said Neuland.

"Sure. I guess it's all been theoretical up to now. Now I'm really going to help kill someone."

"You can sit this one out if you're not ready."

Tilda stood up straight. "Are you kidding? You can't bluff the Skinner with a cigarette lighter. You're going to need someone who can shoot."

"We definitely will."

Going upstairs, she made finger guns at them. "Kapow. Kapow."

Once she was in her room Ford said, “I hope she’s going to be all right.”

“She did fine with Jourgensen,” said Neuland.

“And she really is a good shot.”

“Still. We’re going to have to watch her back.”

“Let’s start her on the.45 tonight.”

“Good idea.”

4

In the evening, after shooting lessons with Ford using the heavy .45, Tilda's arms and shoulders were sore. When they decided to take a break, Tilda went to Neuland's lab and stood behind him.

"I'm sorry," she said. "About what I said earlier."

He turned to her and replied, "It's all right. Really."

She came in and leaned against the end of the worktable. "I wish I could do something to help."

Neuland nodded toward a collection of glassware and said, "You could hand me that green jar."

Picking it up, Tilda said, "This?"

"That's it. Pour ten milliliters into that flask."

When she'd done it, she handed it to him.

"Thank you."

"Is there anything else I can do?" said Tilda.

Neuland handed her a set of heavy rubber gloves. "Put these on. This next part is tricky and I could use another set of hands. Ford is a complete clod in the lab."

After she slipped on the gloves, Neuland handed her a different flask and said, "Now put this on that burner and heat it to exactly one-hundred-and-sixty-five degrees."

"Got it. Can I confess something?"

"Of course."

"I was afraid of you when we met."

Neuland smiled. "That's all right. I was afraid of you too."

"Really?" said Tilda checking the temperature on her flask.

"It's true. I don't generally get along with the rich, especially old money. I didn't trust you. I was ready to fuck off and abandon you and the old man. But you proved me wrong."

"I'm really glad."

"Hand me that pipette, please."

She held up a thin glass cylinder. "This?"

"Perfect," he said and took it from her.

"I'll learn the names soon."

"I know you will."

They worked together into the night.

5

Tilda spent a good part of the afternoon alone on the gun range practicing with the .45. Unlike the 9mm, she had a handful of good shots, but just as many were off-center. Sighing, she left the gun downstairs and went upstairs to have lunch.

Ford and Neuland were already at the table—Ford on his laptop eating a sandwich, and Neuland with a bottle of goofer juice and a book. Both looked up when she came in.

"How's it going down there?" said Neuland.

Pouring herself some coffee, Tilda said, "I'm still pulling to the left. It's driving me crazy."

"The Sig takes a while getting used to. We can work on your stance too," Ford replied.

"Thanks. I want to get better. At everything."

"You're doing great," said Neuland. "Tonight will be fun. We're going to break into a crime scene and have a look around."

"The Skinner's warehouse?"

"Exactly. We might as well get started on this ridiculous job."

Ford said, "We're leaving around two a.m., which should put us there around three. No one is up at three, especially not down at Stony Point."

Tilda set down her coffee cup. "But what if you're wrong and someone sees us?"

"No one will see us."

"But what if they do?"

Neuland took something from his pocket and slid it across the table to her.

It was a square wrapped in leather. When Tilda picked it up it opened like a billfold and she found an NYPD detective badge with her name on the ID card.

"Cool," she said. "A promotion already."

Ford smiled at her. "If any nosy types wander by, just flash that and tell them to fuck off."

Tilda stared at her badge. "Since coming here I sometimes feel like Alice in Wonderland," she said.

"How's that?" Neuland said.

She held up the badge. "I'm a detective now," Tilda said. "It's like Alice said: 'Sometimes I believe in as many as six impossible things before breakfast.'"

Ford held up a Coke can. "Cheers to Alice."

Tilda raised her coffee and Neuland his goofer juice. They all drank together.

At two, they took the subway up to a garage on Fifty-Sixth Street and picked up Ford's black 1972 Pontiac GTO. After getting the keys from the attendant, they sped north on Harlem River Drive to a bridge that took them into the Bronx. After that, they were soon at Stony Point, a patch of land across the East River from Rikers Island.

Finding a spot swaddled in shadows from a warehouse, Ford parked the GTO and they all got out. Tilda followed the men around to the trunk, which was packed with guns and strange equipment she'd never seen before. Neuland handed her an elaborate set of goggles.

"What are these?" she said.

"Night vision. You'll be able to see everything without giving off any light."

"Nice. And what's that you're putting on?" It looked similar to her goggles, but Neuland's rig was much more elaborate.

He said, "A pneumascope. It's like your night vision, but it also highlights signs of organic life."

"And sometimes other stuff," added Ford. "Ready?"

Tilda nodded and put on her goggles. The world suddenly turned very bright and entirely green.

"Let's head out."

The wreckage of the warehouse wasn't much to look at, just a scorched patch of land piled with collapsed sheet metal walls and burnt wooden beams. The only barrier to the site was some tattered yellow police tape on sawhorses surrounding the place. By the tape's battered condition, it was clear that no one had visited in some time. Ford tore it away and they headed out onto the site.

"What exactly are we looking for?" asked Tilda.

"That's the real question, isn't it?" Neuland replied. "We're not sure. Just keep your eyes open for anything interesting. Preferably something that looks out of place."

"Won't the police and fire department and have found everything?"

Ford said, "I trust the fire department more than the cops, but everybody misses things. It's our job to find them."

Tilda picked up a length of pipe and pushed away piles of jagged metal, checking under and around the debris. After a few minutes, she felt a little silly. Through the goggles everything looked pretty much the same. Burned and melted trash. But she kept going even when all she found were dead rat carcasses.

Off to her left, she heard Neuland say, "This is interesting."

She and Ford crowded around him as he held up a broken bone.

"It's part of a clavicle," Neuland said. "The scope reads that it's male."

"Anything else?" said Ford.

"Nothing yet, but I'll take it back to the lab to examine it."

As they split up again Tilda said, "If the Skinner lost this place, it means he's looking for a new one."

"That tracks," said Ford.

"He must have had the place for a long time," said Neuland. "A warehouse this size won't be easy to replace these days."

"Thank god for gentrification," mumbled Ford.

"If the place burned down weeks ago, he might be a bit desperate by now," said Tilda.

"That would be my guess," Neuland said.

"Or it could be something else."

The men stopped what they were doing and looked at her.

"What else could it be, T?"

She shrugged. "I was thinking that maybe since he's back on the street maybe, you know, he likes it. Maybe he got bored with being so careful for so long."

"Shit," said Ford. "I hadn't thought of that."

"I hope you're wrong," Neuland said. "But if you're right, it's going to make him even harder to track down."

"He'll still need someplace to lay low," Ford said.

"Yeah," said Tilda. "A new lair in case running around gets too dangerous."

"Neuland, are you getting any damn thing on the pneumascope?"

"Mostly insects and rats," he said, adjusting the scope's controls. "I'm going to try a reconstruction with the remains of the building and the clavicle."

Ford pulled Tilda back a few yards.

"What's he doing?" whispered Tilda.

"Sometimes the pneumascope can put the scene back together with just bits and pieces of what's there."

"Like a little time machine?"

Ford considered it for a moment. "Yeah. I guess that's a good way to look at it."

Neuland crouched in the debris for a while, then stood and turned three-hundred-and-sixty degrees.

"Holy hell," he said. "Holy hell."

Tilda and Ford went back to him.

"Did you find anything?" said Tilda.

Neuland handed her the scope and said, "Look for yourself."

She removed her night vision goggles and put on the pneumascope. It took her eyes a few seconds to adjust to the staticky image, then she breathed out a quiet, "Wow."

"What did you see?" said Ford.

"The warehouse. It's full of bodies hanging from the ceiling and rafters. Oh god. Some of them are moving. They're still alive. It's like some horrible butcher shop."

She tore off the pneumascope and handed it to Ford, who put it on.

"Well goddamn," he said. "The Skinner was having a grand old time, wasn't he?"

"I'd say so," replied Neuland. He threw the clavicle into the dirt. "I don't think we'll be needing that anymore. We're through here."

Tilda watched it land and said, "Wait. There's something over there. Under that beam."

They went to where she pointed. Tilda dug into the wreckage a few inches.

"Got it!" she said, holding up a water-damaged red book. She opened it as Ford and Neuland looked over her shoulders.

"Can you read it?" said Neuland.

"I think—" she said. "It's pretty burned and waterlogged. I think… Yes. It's something in French."

"Well, fuck us," said Ford. "Who the hell do we know that we can trust and speaks French?"

"I do," said Tilda brightly. "Languages are one of my hobbies. I had a lot of time on my hands back with grandfather."

"You think you can translate it?" said Neuland.

"I'll do my best."

"It might tell us who the Skinner is and why he does what he does."

Ford squeezed Tilda's shoulder. "Nice job. Come on. Let's get out of here before the rats realize they have us outnumbered."

Ford drove them back to Manhattan and they drank through the night to their good fortune.

6

The man lay on his belly in the grass fifty yards from them.

He watched them dig in the ruins of the burned-out warehouse through the telescopic sight on his rifle. To him, they looked like vermin scrabbling through the debris for a meal. Grub eaters. Foul things hunting rotten meat. Or worse, parasites. Yes. He liked that image better. Simple parasites would make everything easier. They were dumb and always hungry.

He watched the three of them through the scope until they finished their work and walked away, eventually vanishing from sight. When they were gone, he disassembled his rifle and headed out. The sun would be up in a few hours and there were arrangements to be made.

7

They woke up late to the sound of someone leaning on the Bunker's front door buzzer.

Gathering around the monitor screen they saw a smiling, heavyset man who scanned the street around him.

"Who's that?" said Tilda.

"Cop," said Ford.

Neuland nodded. "Definitely a cop."

Tilda crossed her arms. "Do you think he's here about last night?"

"I doubt it. We would have seen if there were cameras."

She looked at the screen again. "Maybe Jourgensen and Goss sent him to help us?"

"I doubt it," said Ford. "That's the face of a guy who wants to shit on our floor and expects us to smile about it."

"What are we going to do?"

"Let the fucker in and play it cool. You did great yesterday, T. You can handle this guy."

"You're right. Let the fucker in."

"Here we go."

Neuland buzzed in the smiling man. He wore a dark

Burberry coat and scarf and didn't introduce himself but took his time looking around the room. "Wow. I remember when this was a regular precinct station. I've never seen it so homey."

"It's nice to meet you, officer," said Neuland.

"Detective, actually," said the man, his grin unfaltering. "Fessenden. It's great to meet you all."

Tilda said, "It's good to meet you too, detective. Would you like some coffee? I was about to put some on."

He gestured toward her. "So nice. You don't always meet as nice as her in New York these days."

Ford stepped forward, "Yeah. She's the bee's knees. What is it you want, Detective Fessenden?"

Fessenden looked at Neuland. "You're the dead one, right? A revenant? Is that the right word?"

"That's right," Neuland replied cautiously.

Brightening, Fessenden said, "Wow. I've heard about people like you, but I've never actually met one before. Not that I know of, of course." He laughed at his own joke.

"I'm glad you find my existence so entertaining."

"Oh, I do. All of you. Wildly entertaining. Meeting people like you is what keeps my job interesting."

"That's terrific, detective," Ford said. "But you still haven't said why you're here."

Fessenden walked to a chair where the .45 was hanging from the back in a holster. He took the gun out and sighted across the room.

"A Sig Sauer. You've got to love 'em, right? I have one myself." He opened his coat to reveal a shoulder holster. "Of course, it's a 9mm. They won't let us carry .45s on the street. Bullet might go through a bad guy and hit a poor bystander. Can't have that, right? Too many grieving widows. Too many lawsuits." Again, he chuckled at his joke.

The three others remained silent as Fessenden moved the gun around the room. Finally, he swung it around to point it at Neuland.

"I'd prefer you didn't do that," he said evenly.

Fessenden hesitated a moment before dropping the gun to his side, the smile never leaving his lips. He went to the chair and holstered the .45 before speaking.

"Sorry," said the detective. "I didn't mean to be rude, but that Sig is just so much fun."

Tilda cleared her throat and said, "Are we under arrest?"

Fessenden laughed and waved off the comment. "Arrest? Oh, hell no. It's nothing like that."

"Then why are you here?" said Ford.

Chuckling one more time, Fessenden said, "I thought you would have guessed by now. I want you to kill someone for me."

The three remained quiet for a moment. Then Neuland said, "Why us?"

"Do you mean why I want you to do it or why I don't do it myself?"

"Personally, I'd like to hear both," said Ford.

Fessenden took a step toward him. "All right. I got your names from the friend of a friend. He spoke highly of your services. And, as to why I don't kill this particular person myself, I can't. I'm an officer of the law and the individual I want killed has a high profile in this town."

"Who's that?" said Tilda.

"You ever hear of Andy Vega?"

Ford blinked once. "The art collector guy?"

"Yeah. The art collector guy," said Fessenden lightly. "I want you to kill him for me."

Neuland said, "Why would you want us to kill some crazy rich kid?"

Fessenden held up a finger. "That would be telling. This is a hush-hush kind of situation."

"I'm afraid we don't work that way. You can't buy us to just snuff out any civilian you find annoying."

Raising his eyebrows slightly, Fessenden said, "Is this some kind of hitman code of honor thing?"

"You could call it that," said Ford. "Or a simple 'don't be an asshole' code."

"Then you're turning me down?"

"I'm afraid we have to," said Tilda.

Fessenden pointed to her again. "She's so polite. I love her."

"Polite or not, we're turning you down," said Neuland.

"Even for a hundred thousand dollars?"

Ford frowned momentarily. "Where does a cop get that kind of walking-around money?"

"Detective," said Fessenden.

"Sorry. Where the fuck does a detective get that kind of walking-around money?"

"What did I just say about this being hush-hush? I'm not at liberty to tell you my sources or my reasons. What I can tell you is that I have one hundred thousand dollars with your names on it. Come on, guys. We're all professionals here. Work with me."

Tilda said, "I'm afraid we're already working on another job."

Fessenden stopped smiling and pointed to each of them individually before saying, "So, you're confessing to a New York City police detective that you're engaged in a conspiracy to murder someone?"

Neuland shook his head. "No. You misunderstood her."

"Yeah," said Ford. "We're just redecorating. It's very time consuming."

"I can imagine. A nice place like this," said Fessenden looking around. "But you can't find just a few minutes between looking at swatches to blow Mr. Andy Vega's head off for me? Pretty please?"

"The hundred thousand dollars you mentioned, you have that in cash?" said Neuland.

"You know it. Good American green."

"I tell you what," said Ford. "Let us look into your little venture. Check Vega out. See where he goes. Who he spends time with. Then maybe—"

"You'll try to fit me into your busy schedule?"

"We don't like to go into these things unprepared," Tilda said.

"Sure, sure. That makes sense," said Fessenden. "You work on your feng shui and then look into my offer when you get time. I'll be back soon and we'll finalize things then."

"That sounds fine," Neuland said.

Tilda went to the button that opened the front door. "Thank you for stopping by."

"Thank you, my dear," said Fessenden. He looked at the three of them. "Such nice people. Talk soon."

With that, he went out and disappeared down the street.

The moment Fessenden was gone, Neuland said, "It's a setup."

"Damn right," said Ford.

"You mean he doesn't want us to kill Andy Vega?" said Tilda.

"Oh, he wants Vega dead. but he wants something else too."

"Like what?"

"Fuck if I know."

Neuland said, "The other question is who put him up to this?"

Tilda kept watching the outside monitor. "What are we going to do?"

"Look into it, I suppose," said Ford. "Go through the motions until we can figure out what's really going on."

She turned to them smiling, then shook her head.

"What are you thinking?" said Neuland.

"It's just funny, isn't it? First we had no jobs and now we have two. And we don't want either one."

"I guess that is kind of funny, isn't it?"

Ford sat at the conference table. "I have a headache. Cops give me a headache."

"You're just hungover," said Tilda going into the kitchen. "I'll put on some coffee."

"Fessenden was right. You are the nice one."

She turned and gave him a look. "I do have a gun, you know."

Ford put up his hands in mock fear. "Well, you're not the nice one at all."

"Damn straight," Tilda said.

8

The old grindhouse movie theater on the edge of Greenwich Village was dark, but to his eyes it was as bright as noon.

He'd met the man outside, a junkie shaking in withdrawal and smelling of piss and disease. Under the marquee they'd arranged to meet in the balcony and do their transaction there, implying that he was a drug dealer. He waited by the entrance while the junkie went inside and waited for several minutes. He'd played this game before and knew that dealers always kept customers waiting. It was an unspoken rule of the trade. It kept the buyers soft and pliable, ready to do anything to end their hunger.

He felt hunger too. After killing the woman by the bridge and worrying that he might have been caught on a security camera, he'd grown cautious. Perhaps too much. He felt weak and ached for flesh, any flesh. That's why he chose to debase himself with the street trash in the theater. The man in the balcony needed an easy fix and so did he.

In the lobby, he bought a box of popcorn and headed upstairs. The man he was looking for was seated in the last row of the balcony, at the very top of the theater. There was no one else up there except for a couple—both derelicts—leaning against each other asleep. The air so close to the top of the theater was stuffy and stale. Not a place to linger, so he sat down next to his prey and ate a couple of kernels of popcorn.

The junkie glared at him, whispering, "You smell like the goddamn perfume counter at Macy's."

He ignored the man and stared at the movie screen.

Finally, the prey said, "What the fuck? Do you have the stuff or not?"

He ate a few more kernels. "Do you have money?" he said.

The prey reached into his pocket and pulled out a wad of soggy, wrinkled bills. As he did so, he exposed his wrist. At that moment, the flesh was too irresistible. He'd planned on dragging things out a bit longer, just for the amusement of it, but his hunger overtook him. When the prey shoved the bills at him, he grabbed the man's arm.

As the flesh softened and oozed, drawing away from his body, the junkie tried to scream. The killer clamped his other hand across the prey's mouth and pressed his head into the back wall, letting him twitch and scream silently. He glanced toward the derelicts at the front of the balcony, but they were still asleep and oblivious to everything.

Soon, as the last of his flesh ebbed away, the junkie stopped moving. The killer took deep breaths as his hunger abated and his strength returned. He thought briefly about crushing his prey's skull. It would be quite something for the usher to find—blood and brain matter on the seats—but he decided against it because of the noise. Instead, he set the box of popcorn carefully on the dead man's lap and placed the man's skeletal hand inside as if he was just another filmgoer happily snacking away during the double feature.

He left the theater by a fire exit. The popcorn joke made him chuckle. Yes, it was time to forget about the mistake with the woman and get back into the spirit of things. Have fun again. Maybe he'd even find more prey that night, just to get the sour taste of the junkie's rancid flesh off him.

He walked deeper into the Village, heading into a bar on Christopher Street. It was crowded and the intoxicating scent of drunken revelers filled his lungs. Yes. It was a night for fun.

9

Tilda, Neuland, and Ford sat in the GTO next to Central Park in the Lenox Hill area. Across the street, Andy Vega—short, blond, and dressed in a deep blue Hugo Boss suit—came outside and chatted with his building's doorman until a black limousine pulled up and took him away.

"Swanky," said Ford, revving the GTO's engine.

"So's your car," said Tilda.

"Thanks."

"Can I drive it sometime?"

"If you drive as good as you shoot, sure."

"Awesome."

They followed Vega downtown to a Vietnamese restaurant in SoHo where he had dinner with friends.

Ford frowned. "Well, now I'm hungry."

"We can get delivery when we get home," said Tilda.

Ford and Neuland both laughed softly.

"Wait. What did I say?"

"You said home," replied Neuland. "It's the first time you've used the word."

"I guess it is."

"Welcome to New York," said Ford.

"Thank you."

Ninety minutes later, Vega left the restaurant and got back in the limousine. They followed him to the Financial District, where he left the car and went into a tall glass-walled building housing expensive apartments and lofts.

"Imagine having that kind of money," said Ford.

"I like the Bunker," Neuland said.

"Me too," said Tilda. "I bet none of those places have a gun range."

Ford took out his phone and said, "Wait a minute." After flipping through his address book, he looked back at the building's address. "Amanda Goss lives in this heap. In the penthouse up top."

"Do you think that's where Vega is going?" said Tilda.

"It could be," said Neuland. "She's a well-known art collector."

Ford sighed, "Golly. And we didn't even get an invitation."

"Are we going to sit here and wait for him?" Tilda said.

"Hell no. Come on."

While they waited by the door, Neuland went to the car's trunk and came back with a silver box about the size of a cigarette pack. Placing it on the door, he flipped a switch. A moment later, the lock popped open.

"Neat. Can you teach me to make things like that?"

"Of course," Neuland said.

They went to the elevator and Ford pushed the button for the top floor. The elevator sped them to the penthouse. When Neuland checked the door to Goss's loft, it wasn't locked. They went inside and stood against the wall, trying to blend in with the large, noisy crowd.

After a moment, Neuland said, "There."

Across the room, Vega was staring up at a Roy Lichtenstein painting of a comic book panel while chatting with a tall Japanese woman. A pretty redhead had her arm wrapped around his.

"Who's he talking to?" said Tilda.

"Mariko Ogata," Neuland said. "Goss's lieutenant."

"She's beautiful."

"That she is," said Ford. "She'll also cut off your head and use it to plant daisies."

"Noted."

Neuland said, "Why don't you two get drinks and mingle? Maybe you'll see something useful. I'm going to keep an eye on Vega."

"Sounds good," said Ford as Neuland moved away. When a waiter walked by, he grabbed a couple of glasses of champagne and handed one to Tilda.

Sipping his, he said, "Oh. The good stuff."

Tilda tasted hers and made a face.

"Something wrong?"

She shook her head. "No. I just hate champagne."

"Reminds you of granddad?"

"God no. He was too cheap for the stuff. I just hate wine. Give me rye whiskey."

"Michter's?"

"Angel's Envy."

"Nice."

With drinks in hand, they quietly made a circuit of the room.

"Lot of familiar faces here," said Ford. "Society nobs, a few politicians, and a lot of killers."

"Anyone we should be worried about?"

"All of them."

"I mean, could any of them be connected to Vega in some dangerous way?"

"I wish I knew. Why the fuck does Fessenden have it out for him?"

"Could it be personal?" said Tilda. "Vega seems to be with the redhead but is creeping on other women too."

"I doubt Fessenden would spend a hundred grand on something personal when he could do it himself and frame some street lowlife. No. He wants to stay far, far away from this thing."

When they passed a bar, Tilda set down her champagne and ordered a whiskey. When she turned around, looking for Ford, she found Amanda Goss staring at her not more than a foot away.

"Hello, princess," Goss said. "I don't remember inviting you."

Ford circled back and pulled Tilda a few steps away from Goss. "Hi, Amanda," he said. "Nice shindig."

"I assume Neuland is here too?"

"Right over there."

Goss didn't bother turning. "Aren't you children supposed to be out looking for the Skinner?"

"We are," said Ford.

Goss lowered her gaze slightly and looked up at him. "You seriously think he's here?"

"Here? No."

"Not at all," said Tilda.

"Then why are you at my party?"

"We're following someone who might be connected to him," lied Ford.

"Who?"

Tilda pointed to Vega.

"Andy?" said Goss smirking. "You're insane. Andy's scared of his own shadow."

"Please, just be cool and let us do our job," said Ford.

"No," said Goss firmly. She took Ford and Tilda's glasses and set them on the bar. "Get Neuland and get out of here. And if you ever sneak into my place again, I'll have you shits wiped off the face of the earth. I don't care what you're working on. That goes for you too, princess," she said, glaring at Tilda.

"Okay. We're going. Just don't make a scene and blow our cover," said Ford moving off to retrieve Neuland.

When he was out of earshot, Goss looked at Tilda.

"I don't know how you hooked up with those two, but you could do a lot better than them. I like how you stood up to Jourgensen."

"Thanks. But Ford and Neuland are my friends."

"The kind that will shorten your lifespan by decades."

Tilda hesitated and said, "Are you saying you want to kill me?"

Goss cocked her head slightly. "Princess, killing you would be like kicking a puppy. So, no. I'm not threatening you at all."

Tilda frowned. "If you put it like that, I kind of wish you were."

Goss laughed and pushed her in the direction of Ford and Neuland. "Run along and think about what I said. Watch yourself with those two."

As they walked out of the penthouse, Ford looked at Tilda. "What was Goss going on about to you?"

Tilda drew down the corners of her mouth and said, "Nothing much. Same as you guys. Welcome to New York."

~

They waited in the car for two hours before Vega came outside with the redhead in tow. The limousine picked them up. Ford, Tilda, and Neuland followed them uptown back to Lenox Hill.

When they reached Vega's building, the chauffeur got out and opened the rear passenger door before slamming it shut again. He walked to the front of the car, leaned back and lit a cigarette.

"What was that about?" said Tilda.

Ford half-turned to her in the backseat. "I think Andy and his lady friend are letting nature take its course."

"What?" she said. Then, "Oh gross."

"Who's that?" said Neuland.

"Where?" Ford said.

Tilda pointed. "I see him. Coming out of the park up there."

The figure was a man in a tattered suit, half-hunched over, one arm twisted up before him and the other hanging by his side. He sped from the dark of the park and slammed into the chauffeur hard enough to rock the whole limousine. Using his teeth, he ripped out the driver's throat and bashed the man's dead body against the limousine's windshield until the glass shattered and he fell inside. Before the doorman could grab him, the man slammed the doorman's head back against the building, bursting his skull open in a red spray.

"Groon!" shouted Neuland.

Ford whispered, "Fuck me."

"What's a groon?" Tilda said.

"Later. Get your gun!"

The groon stalked around the car punching out all the windows with a bloody fist. When he punched out the passenger window where Vega and his friend were huddled, he reached inside and tried to grab them. The sound of screaming reverberated down the quiet street.

Neuland circled around the front of the car and Ford around the back. In position, they bolted for the groon and slammed it to the ground—but not for long. The groon crawled back to its knees and hurled Ford onto the roof of the car while tossing Neuland back against the apartment building. When the groon jumped to his feet, he reached back to the car where Vega and the woman were still screaming.

Tilda wondered if she could help the chauffeur, but when it was clear he was dead, she aimed her 9mm at the groon and fired three shots. The groon stepped from the car, looking more surprised than hurt, which gave the redhead just enough time to escape out the passenger side of the car and run down the street. Ignoring her, the groon immediately went back to scrabbling for Vega.

Running around the back of the car, Tilda jumped onto the trunk and fired the rest of her clip down at the groon. Startled again, it fell back and looked down at its bleeding body. With a growl, the groon lunged and tried to grab her legs. Tilda fell backwards onto the front of a parked car as Vega shouted something to her. At the sound of his voice, the groon turned from Tilda, went back to the limousine and began pulling at the locked passenger door. The car rocked back and forth on its shocks: the sound of grinding metal mixed with Vega's screams.

The rocking motion rolled the stunned Ford off the roof of the limousine and down onto the pavement. He pulled himself shakily back to his feet and looked around. Seeing Tilda nervously reloading her gun, he turned to see Neuland running at the groon from behind. Ford leaped, slid across the trunk, and hit the groon at the same time as Neuland. Together, they knocked it back to the ground, but it wouldn't let go of the passenger door handle. As they wrestled with the crazed man, the metal hinges snapped and the door sheared off, falling into the gutter. The groon snapped its jaws wildly, trying to bite them. Tilda opened the passenger door on the other side of the car and shouted, "Vega! Run!" But he just huddled on the floor.

Sprinting around to where Ford and Neuland were wrestling the groon, she could tell they were losing. As hard as they punched and pulled the groon down, it lifted itself back to its feet. Just as it shook the men off and stood upright, Tilda aimed carefully and shot the tattered man once between the eyes. The groon staggered a few steps and finally crumpled to the ground where it lay still.

Vega slowly crawled from the car as Ford and Neuland got back on their feet. The short man looked at them both. "Hey. Weren't you two at Amanda's party?"

Ford pointed to the apartment building and shouted, "Get inside!"

"And don't tell anyone about this," said Neuland.

Without another word, Vega fled into his building, slamming the door shut behind him.

The sound of sirens echoed from somewhere far away.

Ford said, "We need to get out of here."

"One second," said Neuland. He took out a handkerchief, wiped it in the groon's blood and carefully slipped it into his pocket.

Then the three of them sprinted back to the GTO and Ford peeled out before the police arrived.

As they drove down side streets back to the Bunker, Neuland turned to Tilda. "How did you know to do that?"

"Shoot it in the head? I was just trying not to hit you two."

"You did great," said Ford. "That's the only way to kill one of those things."

"What was it?"

"A groon," said Neuland. "A revenant like me, but one that's been poisoned. Someone spiked his goofer juice. The right substance can turn us into babbling fools or, well, what you saw tonight."

"The only way to stop them is get them right between the eyes," said Ford. "A gun. A knife. A fucking swizzle stick. Just something that will reach the brain."

"Are there a lot of them around?"

Neuland said, "No. They don't just happen. They're made by someone."

Ford slammed his hand against the steering wheel. "I knew this was a setup."

"No question about it."

"You think it was Fessenden?" said Tilda.

"Maybe."

"But how does some slob of a cop know how to make a groon?" said Ford.

"We need to check him out," said Neuland.

"We need to fucking shoot him."

"Possibly. But we need to check him out first."

"How do we do that?" said Tilda.

Ford said, "Arsenic Green."

Neuland nodded. "Arsenic Green."

10

While revenant customers lounged on tufted Victorian sofas and padded high back chairs, Arsenic Green served high tea from noon to six p.m. every day, but they didn't actually serve tea.

"It's spiked goofer juice," said Neuland.

Tilda gave him a surprised look. "Like the groon last night?"

"Not at all. If you poison goofer juice with a very specific ingredient you get a groon. But you can just add a few herbs to make it—"

"Revenant moonshine," said Ford. "Everyone in there is getting high. Isn't that right?"

Neuland gave them both a half smile. "It's a pleasant way to spend an afternoon."

"I love it," said Tilda.

They walked a couple of blocks from the car to the tea shop and stopped outside.

"You first," Ford told Tilda.

She looked to Neuland and back to Ford. "Why me?"

"Because it's a women's bar, so it would be better if a woman led the way."

"A revenant lesbian bar, you mean?"

"And their friends," said Neuland. "We're just like anybody else, you know. We have lives and interests. Sometimes we even fall in love."

Tilda took a breath and let it out. "I'm sorry I never thought of that before."

"It's fine. You're still learning your way around our world."

She shook her head once and said, "Okay. I'll walk point. You two behave yourselves."

"Yes, ma'am," said Ford.

Inside, Arsenic Green was dim and cool. Tilda looked around, taking in the Victorian furnishings, expecting to be startled by something that would identify the cafe as a meeting place for the dead. But all she saw were waitresses moving among tables and women enjoying each other's company.

"Wow," she said. "It's really nice in here."

"You learn to appreciate the good things in life when you're dead," said Neuland.

Women turned and stared at them as they made their way further into Arsenic Green. It made Tilda nervous. She didn't know the rules of the place and didn't want to offend anyone.

"What are we looking for?" she said.

"Someone who might know something."

"Who's that?"

"Her," said Neuland.

Tilda followed his gaze to a booth at the back where four elegantly dressed women sipped their drinks and laughed together.

"You're still on point," Ford said to Tilda.

"Right."

She led them to the back of the place where they stood by the table. All four women stopped what they were doing and turned to them.

"Hello, ladies," said Ford.

"Ford," said a tall Japanese woman. "I see you still like crashing parties."

"We don't want to interrupt your afternoon. I promise. We'll only be here a minute."

"Someone time him," said the woman. "Then we have you tossed out."

"Fair enough," said Neuland. "Tilda, I'd like you to meet Mariko Ogata."

"Hi," said Tilda shyly. "I remember you from the party last night." She put out her hand to shake, but Ogata just stared at her. She stepped closer to the table and said, "I heard that you're Amanda Goss's right-hand woman."

Ogata looked at her. "Is that what you heard?"

"Also, that you have a tendency to cut off heads."

"I meant that metaphorically," said Ford.

Tilda shrugged. "Still. It seems like a good way to get your point across."

"It's always worked well for me," said Ogata.

"How do you do it?"

Ogata turned in her seat to get a better look at Tilda. "You're a curious girl."

"I'm new in town and looking for pointers."

Taking a sip of her drink, Ogata said. "I've found an old-fashioned trench cleaver gets the job done. Brass knuckles on one end and a twelve-inch chopping blade on the other."

Tilda balled up her fist. "Must be good for making dinner too. If the tomatoes get sassy, you can punch them in the face."

The other women in the booth laughed, but not Ogata. "Are you the little princess? Amanda told me about you."

"Is that a compliment?"

"Not necessarily."

"Mind if I change the subject a bit?" said Ford.

Ogata turned to Tilda. "Is that all right with you, princess?"

"I'm all ears."

Neuland said, "Do any of you know a police detective named Fessenden? He's quite a bastard, but the smiling type, which makes it worse."

Ogata shook her head. "Never heard of him."

Bo Ligotti raised a red-gloved hand a few inches. "That fool. He's a dirty, brutal prick and a lousy cop. The only reason he even has a job is because he's Jourgensen's cousin. Don't trust a word he says."

"Why do you care about him?" said Ogata.

Ford sighed. "He wants us to kill Andy Vega."

The women laughed at that.

"Little Andy? That's hilarious," Ogata said. "He's as dangerous as a plush bunny."

"Andy must have something he wants."

Ligotti picked up her drink and sipped. Setting it down she said, "Who knows? Assholes like Fessenden don't always need a rational reason. Andy might have bought a vintage G.I. Joe he wanted on eBay or fucked some model he had a crush on."

"I don't think so," said Neuland. "He offered us a lot of money for the job."

Ogata swirled her drink. "That's all we know. We're not responsible for keeping cops off your ass."

"We think he might have sent a groon for Vega last night."

Ligotti shook her head and said, "Fessenden? He doesn't have the balls or wit."

"Or connections, I suspect," said Ogata. "You need to know what you're doing when you make a groon."

"Forget all that," said Tilda. "You still want us to get the

Skinner, right?"

"Of course."

"You people came to us and ordered us to find him or her, but you gave us absolutely nothing to work with. I'm not saying that that's not fair because I know you don't care. What I am saying is that, if you really want us to catch the Skinner, we could do with a little help. Anything at all."

No one spoke for a moment, but then Ogata broke the ice. "I might have heard something."

"What?"

"It's just a rumor."

"We'll take a rumor at this point."

Clearing her throat, Ogata said, "Supposedly, the Skinner smells. Not bad or anything, but he reeks of cologne like some old-time dandy."

"Any type in particular?"

"I don't know men's colognes, but high-end stuff."

Ford said, "My old man used to fucking bathe in Old Spice."

"So, you're saying bad taste runs in the family?"

"We owe you," said Neuland.

Ogata said, "Just find the Skinner and we're even. And bring the princess around when you're done."

"My name is Tilda."

"Well, Tilda, come back sometime and we'll show you things that will blow your mind."

Tilda smiled. "I might just take you up on that."

When they were back on the street, Ford said, "You handled Mariko well back there."

"I like her," said Tilda. "She's... interesting."

Ford looked at her. "Oh man, are you getting a crush on that psycho?"

"You said her cutting off heads was metaphorical."

"Yeah, but I could always be wrong."

"Don't you think she'd be a good connection to have?"

"Yes, but be careful," said Neuland.

"Yes, dad." She glanced at Ford. "Dads."

"Do not even," he said. "Especially if you want to drive the GTO."

"Can I take Mariko to prom in it?"

"This discussion is over."

Tilda looped her arms in Ford and Neuland's. "Thank you both for looking out for me. I think I'm starting to get the hang of things."

"Not until you learn the subways," Ford said.

"Killjoy."

Neuland said, "Are you making any headway with the notebook you found at the warehouse?"

"A lot," said Tilda. "Do you mind if I try some experiments in your lab tonight?"

"Be my guest. What do you think you've found?"

"I don't know. Definitely not an immortality formula, but maybe some kind of precursor."

"Cool," said Ford. "You two work on that and I'll make some more calls about Fessenden."

When they got to the car, Ford tossed Tilda the keys. "Just don't scratch the finish," he said.

Tilda gave a little squeal, and as she slid in behind the wheel she said, "You two sit in the back and watch me go, daddy-o."

"This might have been a terrible idea," said Ford.

Neuland sat back and put on his seatbelt. "We'll know soon."

Tilda turned the car out into traffic.

11

Neuland was in the lab testing the groon blood on his handkerchief when Tilda came in.

"Mind if I try a couple of the Skinner's recipes?" she said holding up the scorched book from the warehouse.

Neuland laughed. "Help yourself to anything in the lab."

"Thanks. How's your work with the groon blood going?"

He submerged a small swatch of the handkerchief in a solution of luminous russula, causing the fabric to curl up and burn along the edges.

"It's very interesting," he said. "There are a few specific substances you can add to goofer juice to create a groon, but this blood appears to be poisoned with something quite rare."

"Is that good?"

"Very. It could help me identify who created the bastard."

"That's exciting."

He nodded in her direction. "What are you working on?"

"I'm not exactly sure," she said, opening the book to a page in the middle. "The Skinner's book refers to a potion that seems to translate as something like 'wolves' eyes'. It's hard to tell exactly because the book is so damaged."

"Good luck with it. You know where everything is."

Tilda put on gloves and eye protection before laying out several vials and flasks on the worktable. She worked slowly, step by step through the smeared pages of instructions. "Man, this stuff stinks," she said after adding sulfur to her potion.

Neuland cut another piece of fabric from his handkerchief. "The joy of experimental alchemy," he said. "You should be in here sometime when I heat up blue amber."

"If it's worse than this, no thanks."

They both worked quietly for another hour. After adding powdered mother of pearl and nirnroot to her mixture, Tilda put it on a Bunsen burner and turned up the flame. She shook her head. "This page is so waterlogged I can't be sure of the exact temperature. Can you read this?"

As she held the book out to Neuland, the beaker on the Bunsen burner sparked and exploded, spraying the hot potion and shattered glass onto Tilda's arms and face, knocking her to the floor. Neuland grabbed a wet rag and wiped as much of the hot potion off her as possible. He knelt down beside Tilda, but when he tried to sit her up, her body went rigid and she shook as if in a deep freeze.

"Ford!"

He came running in and knelt down next to Neuland and Tilda. "What the hell happened?"

"Her potion went bad. Hold her upright while I get something."

Neuland rummaged through his potions until he found a small vial. "Hold her mouth open," he said.

With Ford squeezing the edges of her jaw, Neuland poured the potion down Tilda's throat.

"What is that stuff?" Ford said.

"An elixir to clear the blood of toxins. Until I know exactly what was in the potion she was working on, I can't give her anything more specific without possibly making things worse. Let's get her out of here."

The two men carried Tilda to the sofa in the living room and laid her down with a pillow under her head. Neuland brought in salves to help with her burns and ease her convulsions while Ford took her temperature. "She's got a slight fever," he said.

Neuland put a cold compress on her forehead and checked Tilda's pulse. They repeated this every few minutes throughout the night as Tilda slept.

Around noon she began to move.

"Can I have some water?" she rasped.

Ford looked over at Neuland. He nodded. "It should be all right. I tested her blood and it seems back to normal."

Tilda lay back with her eyes closed as Ford went to the kitchen for water.

"How do you feel?" said Neuland.

"My face hurts. My arms too," she whispered.

"You were burned when your experiment went wrong. Do you remember?"

"I remember that I couldn't read the book, then everything went black."

Neuland touched her forehead to test her temperature. "You're lucky," he said. "The burns are mostly superficial."

Using her elbows, Tilda pushed herself up into a sitting position. "Is the book all right?"

"It's fine. It's right here on the table."

She rubbed her eyes and blinked a few times. Turning to Neuland, she lurched back against the sofa. "What's wrong with you?" she shouted.

"Nothing. I'm fine," he said.

Looking at her hands she said, "Oh god. It's on me too."

"What's on you?"

She stared at her body. "I'm all red and shimmery like I'm on fire. What's happening?"

"You might have hit your head when you fell."

Shaking her head at Neuland she said, "Oh shit. You're kind of gold."

Ford came back and set a glass of water on the table. Tilda stared at him. "You're red too. What's happening to me?"

Neuland sat on the sofa with her and said, "Look at me. Are the colors stable or do they seem to move?"

Tilda swept her hand through the air. "They move. Like I said, kind of like flames but not really."

"Like the aurora borealis?"

"Yeah," she said. "More like that."

"What do you think it is?" said Ford.

"Tilda, I think you're seeing auras," said Neuland. "It's like an energy field that surrounds all living things."

"But you're not alive, and I see you all gold and bright."

"Maybe it works differently for revenants."

Ford sat down next to her. "You're going to be fine."

"Oh," she said. "You just turned purple for a second."

Ford looked at Neuland. "What the hell?"

Neuland thought for a moment and said, "Tell her you like vegan food."

"But I fucking hate vegan food."

"Just say it."

Ford looked at Tilda. "I love vegan food."

She said, "You turned purple again."

Neuland said, "Tilda. I'm a living man named Bob Jones."

"Yep. Purple again."

"That's really interesting."

"What the hell is it?" said Ford.

"If Tilda is seeing auras, she might also sense the tension a body generates when it lies." Neuland looked at her. "If you can see that, you might be able to see other things."

"Like what? I don't like this. I want to go back."

"I don't know if we can change you back. We could consult with someone about the Skinner's book—"

"No," she shouted and grabbed the book from the table. "No one else should see it. It's dangerous. Besides, this is my problem. I'll figure a way out of it."

"You're not going to do it alone," said Ford. "We're going to be there too."

Tilda lay down again and said, "Thanks. Can you turn the lights off? I think I'd like to sleep for a while."

Ford switched off the lights. Neuland pulled all the curtains shut over the windows so the room was nearly black.

"Can you do it now, please?" Tilda said. "I have a headache."

"I just did it."

"No. I can see everything."

Neuland pointed to the light switch. "Turn them on."

When the lights were back on Neuland sat on the table near Tilda. "Look at me," he said. "What do you see?"

"You, but shimmery golden."

Neuland pointed to Ford, who turned the lights off. "What do you see now?"

Tilda looked around and said, "The same. But the room is a little, I don't know. Kind of gray?"

Neuland stood up. "I think we found out what 'wolves' eyes' means."

Ford said, "You think the Skinner can see in the dark?"

"It would give a predator a nice advantage over its prey."

Tilda held her hands up in front of her face. "You mean this is how the Skinner sees?"

"I think so," said Neuland.

"No wonder he's crazy. I hate this."

"Rest. I'll look through my books and see if there's anything helpful there."

"Thanks. I'm really tired."

"We'll be here if you need us."

Ford and Neuland went to the kitchen and spoke quietly.

"You think she'll be all right?" Ford said.

Neuland shook his head. "I have no idea. We'll have to monitor her while I do some research. But I've never seen anything like this before. It might be permanent."

Ford leaned on the counter. "We were supposed to take care of her," he said.

"We're not doing a very good job."

"Why don't you go check your books? I'll stay with T."

"Call me if anything changes."

"You got it."

Tilda slept the rest of the day.

12

A few candles were all that lit the room. Around them were figures frozen in stylized motion, like insects in amber. Fessenden sneezed at the mustiness, dust, and overwhelming smell of cologne.

"Bless you," said the killer.

"Sorry. This place sets off my allergies."

The killer ignored him and slapped at a set of human bones hanging from the ceiling, sending them spinning. "Look at what I've been reduced to," he said. "Scuttling around like a beetle."

He went to stand near Fessenden. When he spoke, the tone was low and seductive. "Not that hunting above doesn't have its allures."

The detective tried to smile. "We'll have you out of here soon," he said. "I have a really good place in mind. A decommissioned police station. It's a goddamn fortress. No one will bother you there. I'll have the owners out soon."

"And how will you do that?"

"Through connections. Freddie Jourgensen—he runs a big syndicate in the city—he has the owners out gunning for you. I'm going to make sure they take the fall for your work."

The killer walked across the room and sat on an old crate. "Were you able to create the groon properly?"

"Oh yeah," said Fessenden proudly. "I slipped some black galena into his goofer juice just like you said and he went wild. Strong as a son of a bitch too. It was hard to handle him. He almost got away from me."

"I'm impressed you found the galena so easily."

"That was through a friend who deals in those kinds of things. But it cost a lot. So, you know, if you could help out with that..."

Again, the killer ignored him, staring at the bones that littered the floor and hung by ropes from overhead pipes. Fessenden sneezed again.

"Sorry."

Finally, the killer said, "Where is the groon now?"

The detective looked away. "It's dead. Ford and Neuland killed it. That little bitch helped."

The killer frowned. "But it followed your plan and killed Vega, yes?"

Shaking his head, Fessenden said, "I'm afraid not."

Picking up a rib from the floor, the killer hurled it at him. Fessenden put up an arm defensively, but it struck the side of his head.

"Sloppy work," shouted the killer. "I don't employ you for sloppy work. Don't let it happen again."

"It won't. I promise. But I had an idea."

"What's that?"

Fessenden walked nervously to the killer. "If you made me like you, I could do my work a lot easier and faster."

The killer gave the detective a kindly smile and lay a hand on his cheek. "Don't fret. You'll be like me in due course. Once I'm back to full strength and have a safe place for my work. By the way, were you able to locate the book?"

"I don't have it, but I think I know who does. I watched them at the warehouse."

The killer frowned. "Good. Get it back. If it didn't burn I don't want it out in the world."

"I'll keep looking." Fessenden fell silent for a moment, then spoke quietly. "Could I have a little more of what you gave me before? It would help a lot."

The killer leaned against the wall. "I met a junkie who spoke that way a night or two ago."

Taking a step back, Fessenden said, "I'm not a damn junkie. I'm trying to help you."

"My apologies," said the killer, waving off the comment. "I simply wanted to remind you not to ask for things you don't need."

"But I do need it. I'm riding herd on gangsters and those hitmen pricks, while still working for the force so no one gets suspicious."

The killer held up his hands. "Calm down. You want a bit more of what you had before? I can help with that." He went to a grimy wooden shelf in the back of the place and took down a vial. "Put out your tongue," he said.

Fessenden crossed the room and did what he was told. The killer used an eyedropper to deposit three small beads of potion onto the detective's tongue.

"Don't swallow. Let your body absorb it. It's more powerful that way."

Fessenden stood in the filthy room trying not to swallow or sneeze for a full minute before he grew dizzy and almost fell over. Grabbing one of the frozen figures, he leaned on it heavily, panting and sweating.

"It's working, I take it?" said the killer.

A few seconds later, Fessenden's head cleared and he stood up. "Yeah," he rasped. "I feel it." He coughed once and his voice returned. "My god. It's wonderful."

"You feel good then."

"Great. Like I could lift a building."

"Excellent. Use what I've given you for good works. You may go now."

"Thank you. But there's just one more thing."

The killer looked annoyed. "You're trying my patience."

"When this is over and you make me like you, well, I don't make a lot of money. Even with the payoffs and a little blackmail here and there, New York is an expensive town."

"Maybe I made a mistake then. Maybe I should offer my gift to someone else and you can move to Nebraska."

"That's not what I meant," said Fessenden quickly. "It's just that I know you're smart and you've stashed away some things." The detective stopped talking and gathered his thoughts. "What I meant is… what's immortality if you're broke?"

The killer clapped his hands and laughed. "That's what you've been stuttering about all this time?"

"Yeah. I guess that's it."

The killer went to Fessenden and put his hands on the detective's shoulders. "When the time comes for you to become like me, you'll have what you wish for. All the gold you want."

"Thank you," he said excitedly. "That's all I wanted to hear."

The killer roughly shoved him away. "Now get out of here and do your job or you'll end up on my dinner table like this other vermin."

Fessenden considered saying something, but seeing the killer's expression he left without a word.

13

Tilda was reading the Skinner's book on the sofa and Neuland was washing glassware from the lab in the kitchen when Ford's phone buzzed. The number came up *UNKNOWN*. Annoyed, he answered it. "Who the hell is this?"

"Hello? I'm sorry to bother you. This is Andy Vega. You're one of the guys from the other night, aren't you?"

"How did you get this number? Never mind. Just fuck off."

"Please don't hang up," said Andy quickly. "I paid a lot of scary people a lot of money to get this number."

"What do you want?"

"I want to give you a million dollars."

Ford set the phone down, put it on speaker, and waved the others over.

"You want to give us a million dollars? What for?"

"For protection. After what happened the other night with that thing."

"A groon."

"Whatever. I almost died, but you saved me. You could have left me there, but you didn't. That's why I want to pay you the money. Will you help me?"

"Sit tight," said Ford and hit the phone's mute button. "What do you think? Is this another setup?"

Neuland rubbed his lower lip. "I don't know. He seemed genuinely afraid for his life the other night."

"He did, didn't he? T, are your eyes still doing that shimmery thing?"

"Yes," she said. "It's driving me crazy."

"I love the Eagles."

Tilda gave him a look. "What are you talking about?"

"Did I turn purple?" said Ford.

"Yes. You were lying."

He looked at Neuland. "We can do that with Vega."

"Get him over here and let Tilda read him?"

"Why not?" said Ford. "What do you think, T? Want to be our lie detector?"

She said, "I don't know if it will work, but I'm willing to try."

"Great. Give me a minute." Ford took the phone off mute. "You there, Vega?"

"I am," came an anxious voice.

"Okay listen, here's how things are going to work. You're going to come over here so we can check you out. But before you move a muscle, we want the first half of the money right now. Consider it a show of good faith on your part."

"What happens to the money if you say no?"

"We'll work that out when you get here. That's the deal. Take it or leave it."

"Where should I send the money?" said Vega.

"I'll text you the info." Ford sent him the bank details and said, "Come alone. You show up with anybody, you don't get in and we keep the money."

"Understood."

"Come over ASAP."

After Ford hung up Tilda said, "Are we really going to do this? We already have two other jobs."

"Except one was definitely a setup," said Neuland.

"Right. And it was about Vega," said Ford. "So, we get him over here and maybe he helps us figure out what the hell is going on."

"That makes sense. But I'm going to keep a gun nearby. I don't want any more surprises."

"I'll get mine too," said Tilda.

Neuland put up a hand. "I don't think Vega is that much of a threat. Besides, this is my job. I kill the living."

Ford said, "And I kill the dead."

"Who do I kill?" said Tilda.

"You're our secret weapon. You kill everybody."

Tilda smiled happily. "Cool."

Thirty minutes later, Vega arrived outside. Neuland checked their bank account. "The money is there," he said.

Tilda pressed the buzzer and let Vega in. The little man looked around awkwardly and said, "Thank you all so much for doing this. You don't know how much better I feel."

"We're glad we could help," said Tilda, stepping behind him.

Neuland said, "Before we go on with anything, we'd like to ask you a few questions."

"Sure."

"Are you Andrew Vega?"

He looked puzzled. "Yes. I called you. I gave you a lot of money."

Neuland and Ford looked at Tilda. She nodded.

"Where were you the night we met you?" said Ford.

"In my car, after Amanda Goss's party."

"Who tried to kill you?"

"I have no idea."

Tilda nodded.

Neuland said, "If we get you through this, can we trust you to give us the other half of the money?"

"Of course."

Nodding again, Tilda gave them a thumbs up.

"Okay. You're in," said Ford. "We'll take your case."

Vega's whole body relaxed. "Thank god. Can I sit down?"

Coming back around him Tilda said, "Of course. Make yourself comfortable."

Vega dropped onto an easy chair. Seeing the Skinner's book on the coffee table he said, "That's an interesting-looking old book."

Tilda picked it up and set it on a shelf. "Thank you. It's very rare. Please don't touch it."

"Sure. Sorry."

Neuland sat down across from Vega. "Let's go through things from the beginning. You went to Goss's party. Did anything odd happen there?"

"Nothing. I just had drinks with some friends. And I met Angie."

"Who's she?"

"She's who I was with when that lunatic attacked us."

"The redhead?" said Ford. "Where is she now?"

Vega pursed his lips. "Heaven. Maybe. Angie had the worst luck. First, she got attacked with me and then she was shot by a mugger yesterday."

"Yeah. That is bad luck. Did anything strange happen with her at the party?"

"Nothing. Except she made a phone call before we left and seemed a little funny afterwards."

"Funny how?"

"Tense."

"That's interesting. But it still leaves us with the questions, why would someone want to kill you and who?"

"Really, I have no idea."

"Do you know a police detective named Fessenden?" said Neuland.

"Never heard of him. Who is he?"

"He offered us a hundred thousand dollars to kill you," said Ford.

Vega stood up, going pale.

"Sit down. We were never going to do it."

Tilda said, "We just followed you to see why Fessenden wanted us to."

Sitting down again Vega said, "What did you decide?"

"That the whole thing was a setup. But not for you. For us," said Neuland.

"Why would someone do that?"

Ford shrugged. "Probably the groon was supposed to kill you and we were supposed to take the blame."

"But why me?"

"You really want to hear my theory?"

"Please."

"That groon would have ripped you apart, so people would probably think the Skinner did it. You're high profile enough that you'd get headlines but also—and sorry, man—other than that you're kind of, well, not significant. Your death would fuck us up but not actually change anything else in the world."

Vega dropped his hands into his lap and laced his fingers

together. "Yeah. I know what you mean and it kind of fucks me up," he said. "I was never good with people. When I inherited the money I used to think you could buy friends. Turns out you can only rent them, and not for very long. When the party's over everybody leaves, and no one calls unless they want something."

"I'm sorry," said Tilda. "Of course you can stay."

"Seriously?" said Vega looking around.

"Don't get too excited," said Ford. "There are rules. There's an air mattress in the basement. You can sleep there. You can also hang out up here. In fact, do whatever you want but keep quiet and don't get in the way. If you want to stay alive, we have a lot of work to do."

Tilda spent the day with a French dictionary and the Skinner's book. In the evening, she slammed the book shut and said, "Shit."

"What is it?" said Neuland.

"The Skinner is definitely a he, which doesn't thrill me," she said. "I was hoping for an evil ice queen. He's an alchemist and he's used a lot of names over the years, but when he wrote this book he was calling himself Jean-Pascal Bacri."

"What else?"

"Believe it or not, he seems to have found the key to immortality."

"What do you mean?" said Ford.

"I mean just what it sounds like. But his immortality is messy. He doesn't stay young forever. He has to renew himself. He gets old. He can even get sick. When he does, he needs other people's flesh to replace his own. He kind of absorbs it somehow, which is why the police keep finding bones at the death scenes."

"Oh god," said Vega. "That's who's after me?"

Tilda went on. "He's probably killed thousands of people over the years and he'll keep killing forever."

"Thousands?" said Neuland. "How is that possible?"

"He's moved around a lot. And he's *really* old."

Ford said, "Can you narrow that down?"

"Like King Tut old." She shook her head. "No wonder he's crazy. There's something else too, and it's scary. From what I could make out, I'm not sure he can die. After all this time he's too powerful. You can hurt him but killing him might not be an option."

"Well, I'm fucked," said Vega looking around. "How can you stop someone who won't die?"

"Everything dies," said Ford. "Some things just go down harder than others."

Tilda opened the book to the last few pages. "It looks like Bacri learned a lot of his alchemy from a book belonging to a Roman cult that worshipped someone named Abaddon."

"Who's that?"

"A fallen angel," said Neuland.

"You think an angel taught him this shit?" Ford said.

"No more than I believe in the Dagon cult's sea monster. But the cult believed and seems to have discovered something."

Vega leaned forward on his elbows. "The Roman book you're talking about. Do you mean an Abaddonian codex?"

"Maybe."

Vega hesitated for a moment, then said, "I have one of those."

Ford stood up. "Are you fucking serious? Why?"

"I saw it at auction," said Vega. "It was very pretty."

"I might have to murder you after all."

"And it was a good investment," said Vega.

"That isn't helping."

"Where is it?" said Neuland.

"At my apartment. But I have to get it. The safe is fingerprint protected."

Ford said, "We could just cut off your hand."

Tilda put her hand on Vega's and said, "He's just kidding."

Vega didn't speak again.

"Before we go," Tilda said, "I'd like to ask for samples of everybody's blood."

"Why?" said Ford rubbing his arm. "I hate needles."

"It's an experiment from the book."

"You want to go back to the lab so soon after your accident?" said Neuland.

She nodded her head firmly. "Absolutely."

"Okay," said Ford. "Everybody roll up your sleeve. You too, Vega."

"Is this going to help stop the alchemist?" Vega said.

"I hope so," said Tilda. "We'll know more when we get the codex."

14

In the evening, as they prepared to go to Andy Vega's apartment, Ford said, "How comfortable are you feeling with the .45, T?"

"A lot better. I've been practicing."

"Great. Leave the 9mm and take the Sig."

Vega sat on the sofa out of the way as everybody else got ready. "Wait. She said you can't kill him."

"We'll just have to see," said Neuland.

Gesturing for Vega to join them by the door Ford said, "Remember to stay back, and don't ask questions."

They drove the GTO uptown to Lenox Hill. When the group approached Vega's building, the new doorman tipped his hat to him. Vega just ducked his head and refused to meet the man's gaze.

Tilda said, "It's okay. What happened with the doorman the other night wasn't your fault."

"I still feel rotten."

"Want to feel better? Find his family and pay for the funeral," said Ford.

"I never thought of that."

"The rich never do," said Neuland as he pressed the button for the elevator.

When the door opened on Vega's floor, they left him in the car and went into the hall with their guns out. Satisfied the corridor was clear, Ford waved Vega out of the elevator and they hurried to his apartment. Once Vega unlocked the door, Neuland pushed him aside and went in first. The lights came on, but the apartment remained quiet.

"Neuland. You all right?" called Ford.

"Not really, but the room is clear. Come in."

Ford stepped inside and said, "Holy shit."

Tilda brought Vega in by the arm and made a face. "It looks like grandfather's house, but—"

"Like a toy store too?"

"Yeah."

The off-white walls rose up to a decorated pressed tin ceiling twenty feet overhead. The vast room in which they stood was like a very peculiar museum, full of paintings, Greek and modern sculptures, shelves of rare comics, shining gadgets both large and small, and polished antique furniture butting up against Eames chairs. A row of Brabbu stools fronted a full-size restaurant bar against one wall. Liquor bottles glowed before an amber lighting fixture as long as the bar itself.

Ford looked round. "I see a lot of stuff, but I don't know. What exactly is it you collect, Vega?"

"Things I like. Things of beauty that need protection and love," he said defensively. Then, "Listen. I don't criticize you for living in a damn missile silo, so don't criticize my home."

"Fair enough."

Tilda went to a shelf of antique books. "I love these. Are those all Dickens?"

Vega stood next to her. “First editions. Yep. I have every title. Even a signed one.”

“And that painting,” she said. “Is it a real Paul Delvaux?”

Vega shook his head at it. “Yeah. My father bought a lot of his stuff. I don’t get the surrealists at all. I think my father only liked it because of all the naked women.”

“How much is all this worth?” said Ford.

“I have no idea. Great-grandma started the collection in England and shipped the original work over.”

Neuland turned in a slow circle and said, “It’s Xanadu.”

“What’s that?”

“It’s from Citizen Kane. An empty house full of beautiful treasures.”

“Hey,” shouted Vega. “Why are you all up my ass so much?”

Neuland said, “People like us don’t register to people like you until the world is on fire. At best we’re janitors or landscapers. A necessary evil.”

“I’m paying you well, so you can back off.”

“You want some respect?” said Ford. “When you pay for the doorman’s funeral, find out if he had kids and pay for their college.”

“Do that and we’ll bring you chocolate cake on your birthday,” said Neuland.

Tilda went to Vega. “Why don’t you take us to the safe?”

The small man brightened. “You’ll love this. I designed it myself.”

They followed him to a large antique wardrobe in the back of the apartment. Opening it, Vega slid the clothes away and pushed open the rear panel. “Welcome to Narnia,” he said.

“You’re insane,” said Ford.

Tilda stepped inside the wardrobe and poked her head out the back. “I think it’s adorable. I want one too.”

Vega turned to Ford and Neuland. "I like her."

"Can you show us the safe now?" said Neuland.

"Can just Tilda come?"

"Sure," said Ford. "We'll keep guard in here."

Vega led her into a bare back room with a vault door set against one wall.

"I like this. Very space age," she said.

"Thank you. Before I open the vault, would you mind turning around?"

"Of course."

She listened as Vega worked a mechanical lock until he hit the right combination. "Okay," he said.

Tilda turned around as Vega put his hand on a bright glass plate. Once the scan was complete, the bolts on the vault pulled back with a *clunk* and he opened the door.

"Oh my god."

"You like it?" said Vega proudly.

"It's amazing."

Shining bullion was neatly stacked in one corner. Rare jewelry sat in display cases and on dresser's dummies. A DaVinci leaned against a pile of cash. The codex was in the far back of the vault on a lectern. Vega retrieved it and handed it to Tilda.

"Please be careful. I don't know if there's another one in the whole world."

The codex was heavy, the size of a Gutenberg Bible and bound in leather. The cover was trimmed with gold leaf and precious stones. Inside, the pages were highlighted with illuminations and notes in the margins.

They went back through the wardrobe to the main room. Vega said, "I should have mentioned before. I'm afraid the codex is in Latin."

"Yeah. That would have been nice," said Ford.

"It's okay," said Tilda calmly. "I had twelve years of Catholic school. I know my way around an ablative noun or two."

"Great. Can we get started?" said Vega.

"Right when we get back to the Bunker."

"Wonderful," said Vega gently taking the book from her hands.

As the four of them headed for the door, the lights flickered once, twice, and went out. Neuland shoved Vega back into the wardrobe. "Get inside and stay quiet."

Ford, Tilda, and Neuland fanned out across the room. Banging his knee into a chaise-lounge, Ford cursed and said, "T, can you see anything?"

"Yes. It's fine. Nothing is different."

"We're pretty much blind, so you're in charge."

"Don't worry. I've got this," she said. Then, "By the window!"

Glass exploded into the room as a man's silhouette burst inside and jumped down into the dark. Neuland and Ford opened up with their guns, shooting a wide pattern where the silhouette had come down.

To Tilda, the intruder glowed a bright cyan that vibrated rather than shimmered, leaving a smeared trail in the dark when he moved. He slammed into both Ford and Neuland, knocking them to the floor.

"It's him. Bacri," shouted Tilda. "Stay down."

As she watched, the alchemist circled the room, getting closer to the wardrobe. Taking careful aim, she shot into the center of the blur, but he was too fast. Four shots missed, but when he was making his way around the bookcase, kicking Ford and Neuland out of the way, Tilda's fifth shot spun Bacri around so he stumbled into an antique table. She kept shooting until he fell to his knees.

"I'm out of bullets," Tilda shouted.

Neuland managed to get out a small flashlight and pin Bacri in a circle of illumination.

Ford shot at him but, even bloody and wounded, the alchemist was still able to streak away. Neuland dived behind the bar, grabbed a bottle of vodka, and shot at Bacri. When he ran at him, Neuland broke the bottle on the side of the alchemist's head and sparked his lighter, tossing it at the man. Bacri burst into flames and stumbled backwards, falling over furniture and sending sculptures crashing to the floor. When he made it back to the window, he grabbed the edge of the shattered sill and jumped outside, a blazing star falling out of sight. As soon as the alchemist was gone, the lights flickered and came back on.

Tilda went to the wardrobe and said, "You can come out now, Andy. He's gone."

Vega crept into the room and looked around. "Was that Bacri?"

"I think we can assume that," said Neuland.

"How did he know where I was hiding?"

Ford limped over, wiping blood from his lip. "The fucker was probably watching us through your window the whole time."

Vega looked at around, surveying the damage to his apartment. "My poor collection."

"Is the apartment soundproof?" said Neuland.

"No."

"Then let's get going," Ford said. "Before some solid citizen calls the cops."

"What about Bacri?"

Tilda said, "He's hurt. He won't be bothering us again tonight."

Vega held the codex tight to his chest as they drove back downtown, weapons reloaded and within easy reach.

15

When they reached the Bunker, Vega went straight downstairs to lie down in the shooting range. "Leave the codex," said Neuland. Vega set it on the coffee table before trudging away.

More shellshocked than scared, thought Tilda. She sat on the easy chair across from the sofa and said, "I shot someone tonight."

"You okay?" said Ford.

She looked at him. "I don't know. I'm horrified at myself, but kind of giddy at the same time."

"Yeah. That's pretty much your first shoot."

"Do you think—?"

"That he's dead?" said Neuland. "Doubtful. You said it yourself. He'll be hard to take down. If we can at all."

Tilda sat back and hugged herself. "But he's hurt, right? We at least hurt him?"

"Absolutely."

Ford said, "Being shot and set on fire is going will ruin anyone's evening. Even someone immortal."

"The downside of that is that he's wounded. He'll have to kill again soon to restore himself," Neuland said.

"Maybe more than once, just to be a dick."

Tilda set her gun on the coffee table, pulled the codex onto her lap and opened it. After leafing through a few pages she said, “This really is beautiful.”

“But is it helpful?” said Neuland. “I think we’re in serious trouble if it isn’t.”

Tilda smiled up at him. “Don’t worry. I’m not letting it out of my sight and I’m reading every single word.”

“Let us know if there’s anything you need.”

“A drink? Something to help me calm down?”

“You got it,” said Ford grabbing a bottle of rye from the shelf and pouring a good amount into a tumbler.

“*Gratias tibi*,” she said when he handed it to her.

“Latin?”

“*Sic*. Yes. I’m just trying to shift my brain over into the right reading mode.”

“We’ll leave you alone and let you work,” said Neuland.

A few hours later, as dawn began to filter into the room through the windows, Tilda stretched and went into the kitchen to make coffee.

Ford was asleep on the sofa, but Neuland came in from his lab. “Did you find anything interesting?”

Tilda nodded as she poured water into the coffeemaker. “A lot. I mean, a lot.”

“Have you found a way to kill him?”

She frowned as she set the coffeemaker brewing. “Not yet. But I know some things he tries to avoid.”

“Such as?”

“He sure doesn’t like revenants. He might even be afraid of them.”

Neuland nodded a little and said, "That makes sense. We could remind him of what he's running from."

"That's what I was thinking." She got down two coffee mugs from the cabinet. "There are some interesting spells in there too. Curses. Potions. Self-defense. It's fascinating."

"Maybe you'll translate some of it for me when this is over."

"I'd like that."

Ford stirred on the sofa and sat up. "Did I fall asleep? What did I miss?"

"Nothing," said Tilda bringing him a cup of coffee. "I've been reading and Neuland has been in the lab."

Taking a couple of sips of coffee, Ford said, "Sorry to leave you in the lurch. But I'm up now. What can I do to help?"

"Nothing right now. Everything is fine."

"I suppose we should check on Vega. I don't think he's handling all this well," said Neuland.

"I'll do it," said Ford. "Give me a chance to stretch out a little."

"Don't scare him," said Tilda.

"I'll be a gentle little lamb." But when he was halfway down the stairs he shouted, "Vega! You still alive down there?"

When he came back up a few minutes later, Neuland said, "How's Vega?"

Ford gave him a thumbs up. "He's curled up like a pill bug on the mattress, but he's not insane or dead, so I count that as a win for everyone."

"Poor guy," said Tilda. "All he wanted was a date at the party, and all he got was the groon, Bacri, and us."

"Hell of a night for anyone."

"For all of us," said Neuland before returning to his lab. When he finished his coffee, Ford went to join him while Tilda read more of the codex.

At nine the door buzzer went off.

"Fucking Fessenden," said Ford looking at the security screen.

"Do we let him in?" said Tilda.

Neuland came up behind her. "We should see what the bastard wants."

Ford pushed the entry button and Fessenden came inside. He walked to the middle of the living room and gave them the same warm grin he gave them the first time they met. "So," he said finally. "Here we are again."

"What can we do for you, detective?" said Neuland.

Fessenden's smile faltered slightly. He held out his hands in front of him. "No. It's what can I do for you."

"What can you do?" said Ford.

"Not having you all killed for one thing. I won't even bother mentioning jail to people like you. I respect you too much."

"That's swell. Thanks."

Bringing his hands together, Fessenden lowered them in front of him. "But I have to admit, I'm really disappointed in all of you. I thought you were pros. From what I hear, Vega is still alive. And you're leaving messes all over town."

"Which messes are those?"

"Don't be cute. Why isn't Vega dead?"

"Don't worry about Vega. He's off the streets and won't be bothering anyone."

"Where is he exactly?"

"Where he can't hurt anybody."

"And nobody can hurt him," said Tilda.

Fessenden took an exaggerated breath. "That wasn't our deal."

Ford said, "The way I remember it, we didn't actually have a deal. You offered us money but included a lot of veiled threats."

For the first time, the detective looked angry. "My threats

aren't veiled. When I threaten you, you'll know it. Now I'm asking again, where is Vega?"

"Who?" said Neuland.

Fessenden looked around the room. He stared at Tilda. "He's here. Isn't he? I want to see him."

"You're not killing anyone in our home," she said.

"So, he is here. Why?"

"He has information we need," said Neuland.

"Information? About what?"

Ford said, "The Skinner."

Fessenden looked around again. "See? This is what I'm talking about. I didn't hire you to worry about the Skinner."

"Like I said, you didn't hire us at all."

"Who told you about Vega being alive?" said Neuland.

"I read the report about what happened at his apartment last night. A break-in that turned into the fucking OK Corral. There was blood, but no bodies. It stands to reason that it was you in there with him."

"Really? How did we get in?"

"The front window was busted all to hell."

Ford laughed. "Do you really think we go flying into buildings like Batman?"

"I don't know what you fuck-ups do," Fessenden growled.

"How's Angie?" said Tilda.

The detective turned to her. "Who?"

"She was with Andy at the party and they went home together. She was with him when the groon attacked."

"A groon? What's that? It sounds scary."

Tilda stared at him for a few seconds longer, then said, "You're lying. You know what a groon is. And Angie made a phone call before leaving the party. Was that to you?"

"Who the fuck is Angie?"

Turning to Ford and Neuland she said, "He's still lying."

"Angie's dead," said Ford.

"Allegedly shot by a mugger," Neuland said. "But you wouldn't want anyone knowing that you were the one she called."

"Except your employer."

Fessenden shrugged. "NYPD doesn't pay me to kill random redheads."

"How do you know she's a redhead?" said Tilda.

"And we don't mean NYPD," said Neuland. "We mean your real employer."

Fessenden pulled his pistol from under his coat and pointed it at Tilda. "Fuck you, and fuck you, and fuck all of you. Bring me Vega or I'm shooting her in self-defense."

Ford said, "How's your boss doing this morning? A little crispy on the outside? I bet that fall really hurt."

"You never cared about Andy," said Tilda. "You just wanted the codex for the alchemist."

"And to make us look like we were involved in Vega's death," said Neuland.

Fessenden raised his eyebrows slightly. "I *will* shoot her."

"My name is Tilda."

"Fine. I will shoot you, Tilda."

Ford said, "Do you really think you can kill all of us before we make you eat that gun?"

The detective's grin returned. "Yeah. I do." He gave a chair a light kick and it flew across the room, smashing to pieces against the far wall. He flicked his hand back and gouged a deep hole in the concrete wall. "See? He's already given me some of his power. I'll be just like him soon."

Ford, who'd removed his gun before lying down the night

before, made a feint toward the weapon. This gave Neuland, who was still armed, a chance to pull his pistol and shoot Fessenden. The detective slammed back against the wall but didn't fall. He raised his gun and shot back, hitting Neuland twice in the chest. Ford scrambled to the coffee table to get his pistol, but Fessenden got off another shot, hitting Ford in the arm. Spinning, he kicked the coffee table at Neuland, knocking him to the ground. The detective pinned him there with a foot on the table and said, "I know it's hard to kill your type, but what happens if I empty this whole clip into your brain? Let's see."

"Detective!" shouted Tilda, holding her hands in the air.

Fessenden kept the gun on Neuland but turned to look at her. "I haven't forgotten about you, sweetheart. I'm just dealing with the adults first."

Tilda shouted a long string of Latin at him and the detective smiled. "What the fuck was that?"

She kept shouting until Fessenden's face slipped from a grin into a deep scowl. "Stop that," he said, shaking his head.

Tilda kept repeating the words. Fessenden pointed his gun at her. She walked toward him, shouting the words over and over. The tension in the detective's body slowly began to ease. His shoulders sagged as he gradually turned the pistol and pressed it to the side of his head.

"Stop it," he said through gritted teeth.

Tilda shouted once more.

"You bitch," said Fessenden just before he blew his brains out.

Neuland crawled out from under the coffee table as Ford, his arm covered in blood, said, "What the fuck was all that?"

Tilda ran to him. "It's a curse from the codex. I didn't know if it would work, but I couldn't reach my gun. I had to do something."

"Good thinking."

Neuland and Tilda picked up Ford and set him on the sofa. Then Neuland dropped down next to him, black fluid leaking from the bullet holes in his chest. "There's a bottle of goofer juice on the kitchen table. Would you get it for me?"

Tilda grabbed the bottle and handed it to Neuland, who downed the whole thing.

"That's better," he said, slowly rising to his feet and going to his lab. He came back with a leather satchel and set it on the sofa between himself and Ford. "Open it," he said to Tilda.

When she did, she found a selection of surgical instruments. She immediately shook her head. "For the bullet? No way. I don't know anything about that."

"It's all right. I'll talk you through it."

"Do it fast, okay?" said Ford, his face white and covered in sweat. "I'm not feeling so great."

"Don't worry. You're getting knocked out," said Neuland.

"Yes, please."

Neuland drew some sedative from a small bottle into a syringe and injected Ford. The man was unconscious in a few seconds. "You're going to have to do the rest, Tilda. My hands are too shaky for surgical work right now."

She nodded her head firmly twice and said, "What do I do?"

"Take out the retractor. It looks like an odd pair of scissors."

After a moment of looking, Tilda removed a silver object from the bag. "This?"

"Perfect. Slowly put the blades into Ford's arm and squeeze the handles to hold the wound open."

Tilda did as she was told, though Ford's flesh parting made her feel nauseous. "Oh god. There's a lot more blood now."

"There's a bottle of saline. Use that to wash it away. Can you see the bullet yet?"

"Yes. It's not too far in. Just under the skin."

"Good. Now look in the bag again. Do you see something that looks sort of like large tweezers?"

"I have them," said Tilda.

"Just reach in slowly and extract the bullet. Use the saline to wash the blood away if you can't see it."

Working the slender metal into Ford's arm, Tilda bit the inside of her cheek until it bled. "Shit!"

"What's wrong?"

"I missed and now it's in deeper."

"Stay calm and try again. You can do it."

Once more, Tilda washed Ford's blood away and reached into his wound. A few seconds later, she felt the silver tines close around something hard. She pulled back slowly and the bullet slid from Ford's arm before clattering to the floor. "I did it!"

"Perfect. Now pack the wound with gauze while I get ready to sew him up."

Tilda watched Neuland close and suture Ford's arm. The goofer juice must have taken effect, she thought, because his movements were quick and precise.

He's done this before, she thought. *A lot. Poor guy.*

When Neuland was done, they both sat down again, exhausted. Tilda said, "Aren't you going to take out the bullets that hit you?"

Neuland waved an exhausted hand at her. "I will. But later."

For several minutes everything was quiet. Then Tilda said, "I killed someone today. It feels a lot different from just shooting a person, huh?"

"It does. But he would have killed us all. You saved us."

"I know, but I don't feel very good. Kind of nauseous."

"A lot of that is adrenaline. Relax. It will come down soon."

"Part of me wants to cry, but another part—I don't know."

"The other part is relieved you're alive and grateful that you took action."

"Yes. I guess I am. I used to be too afraid to do anything at all."

"And now look at you," said Ford.

Tilda narrowed her eyes at him. "How long have you been playing possum?"

"Not long. I just heard the last bit. Neuland's right. You saved us."

A quiet voice came from the kitchen. "Is it over? Is everyone okay?"

"Hi, Andy. You can come in," said Tilda. "Everyone is fine."

He slowly came into the living room. "It doesn't look that way."

"Hush," said Ford. "Pour us drinks, and one for yourself. We survived Bacri and his bootlicker."

Vega brought them all shots of whiskey. They toasted each other and drank them down.

"What about the body?" Vega said.

"That's mine," said Neuland. "Help me carry it into the lab."

"I'm going to be sick."

"The bathroom is over there."

Neuland and Tilda worked into the afternoon, examining Fessenden's body and clothing. Around two, Tilda went out to bring Ford into the room. "What's the story?" he said.

Neuland took off his eye protection and said, "Everything about Fessenden is ordinary, except for his blood. I want to study it and compare it to what Tilda learned from the codex. I'm going to use some of the blood Tilda drew yesterday."

"Okay," said Ford. "But how is that going to help us find Bacri?"

"It's not. I'm going to have to try something a bit more radical," Neuland said examining the vials containing their blood samples. "I hope Fessenden's brain isn't too damaged for it to work."

Ford made a face. "Oh man. You're going to do the thing with the other thing, aren't you?"

"I'm afraid so."

"Count me out. I can't stand the smell."

"I know. Tilda, will you help me?"

She looked nervously from Ford to Neuland. "Of course."

"You're braver than I am, T, to play with what Neuland's got planned. Good luck." Ford pulled Vega out of the room. "Come on. Let's get drunk."

When they were gone, Neuland handed Tilda a pair of thick rubber gloves and said, "Help me set Fessenden upright in that chair over there."

As they struggled with the detective's limp body, Tilda said, "What exactly are we going to do to him?"

Once Fessenden was upright, Neuland clamped the back of his head to keep him in place. "Do you believe in the soul?" he said.

Tilda thought for a moment. "I'm not really sure. I saw a lot of strange things back at Pale House and here, but I just don't know."

"That's all right. To answer your question, we're going to try and capture a little bit of someone's soul. Hopefully, a bit of two souls."

"How do we do that?"

Neuland picked up a bottle and said, "Have you ever worked with cyanide?"

16

They closed the lab door and placed duct tape around the edges to seal it off from the rest of the Bunker. "We don't want the fumes getting out," Neuland explained.

Tilda finished the taping while Neuland brought out an old bellows camera from the closet. He set it up from across the room and took his time focusing the lens on Fessenden. When he was done, he went back to the closet and retrieved a large curtain of a scratchy, woven material. "Help me hang this up? There's a ladder over there."

Neuland held up the curtain and Tilda looped the top over several hooks embedded in the ceiling so that it hung down behind the dead detective. When she was done she said, "What is this?"

"I got it from a friend in New Orleans," Neuland said.

"Yes, but what's the material? It doesn't feel like wool."

He thought about it for a moment before answering. "I suppose if you're going to assist me, you should know the truth about the things I work with."

"Now you have to tell me," said Tilda.

"Have you heard of a Hand of Glory?"

"Sure. It's a dead man's hand you can use to do magic."

"Close enough," said Neuland. "This is similar to a Hand of Glory. It's woven from the hair of dead men. Men who've been hanged." He paused. "It's very old."

Tilda climbed down from the ladder and looked up at the curtain. "That's a lot of dead men."

"It is. That's why it's so rare and valuable."

"What do you use it for?"

"Hopefully, it will let us capture a soul, or least get a glimpse of one."

"Cool. What do we do next?"

"We're going to be making a modified version of a cyanotype. That means working with some dangerous chemicals, so put these on," Neuland said. To go with the gloves he'd given her earlier, he handed her a rubber apron, a set of goggles, and a small respirator that she slipped on over her face.

After they both put on their gear, Tilda said, "You mentioned cyanide. What else are we using?"

"Ferric ammonium citrate," he said. "That's why we have respirators."

"Do you breathe?"

"No, but I still don't want the chemicals on my skin or going up my nose. It makes me itch."

"Sorry. So, how does all this work?"

"We're going to coat some special paper with the ammonium citrate and cyanide. Then, I'll take a photo and expose the glass plate with a drop of Fessenden's blood. If everything works out the way I hope, we'll have our souls."

"Is there anything else I can do before we get started?"

"Yes. Flip that switch on the wall. It activates a fan that vents the fumes outside."

Tilda did as she was told and they checked their equipment

one last time. After they carefully coated the paper in the poisonous chemicals, Neuland dimmed the lights, leaving a single red bulb illuminating Fessenden. Then, slipping a glass plate inside the camera, he triggered the shutter with a release at the end of a short length of wire. Tilda counted under her breath as Neuland waited for the shutter to close.

"Twenty-eight, twenty-nine, thirty, thirty-one—" She finally heard the click.

Neuland took the plate from the camera and exposed it with a mercury vapor lamp. Slowly, an image began to emerge on the blue-tinted paper. Tilda could just make out a man: Fessenden. But he was whole again, his face undamaged by the gun shot. There was a thick fog around his body that wisped along the back of the photo. It was another figure, ghostly and vaporous. It hovered over Fessenden's shoulder with its hands raised. Tilda couldn't tell if it was gesturing at something or about to strike the dead detective. Over several minutes the forms solidified enough for her to recognize the second figure as the alchemist. He stood before an elaborate backdrop that she couldn't identify. And she saw something that she thought could be a Ferris wheel in the far distance.

"Is that really Bacri?" she said.

Neuland held up the photo. "It has to be. When Fessenden said that Bacri had given him some of his power, I had a feeling that their souls might have mingled. And it looks like I was right."

Tilda got closer to the photo, scanning the details. "What does it all mean? Will it help us find him?"

Smiling, Neuland said. "I'm sure of it. Would you bring the others in and I'll explain. Oh, and throw that shroud over Fessenden? It's treated with a potion that will preserve him for a while."

"Thank god," she said. "Staring at him was really creeping me out."

"Sorry. We'll get rid of him soon."

"I'll bring in the others."

Going into the living room, Tilda was relieved to take off her protective gear. "It worked," she said.

Ford got up and grinned. "I knew you could do it. But you look a little beat up. Want a drink?"

"Very much."

He poured her some rye and Vega said, "What's that smell?"

"Cyanide and ammonia," said Tilda. "It's messy communing with the dead. But the vent will clear out the fumes in a few minutes."

Vega crossed his arms in front of him. "You people have a hell of a job."

"And we're getting well paid for it. Isn't that right, Andy?" said Ford.

Gesturing with his hand, Vega said, "I haven't forgotten. If I'm alive at the end of this, you'll get the rest of your money."

"Cheers to that."

Tilda finished her drink. "I think it's probably safe to go in now. Come on, Andy. You should see this."

"No fucking way," he said. "I collect books. You people go and commune with the dead."

"Suit yourself," said Ford. "Come on, T. Let's go see the magic show."

Neuland was studying the photo with a magnifying glass when they entered the lab.

"How's it look?" said Ford. "T said the shot came out well."

"Better than I'd hoped," Neuland said holding the photo up for them. "Look at this. What do you see?"

Ford squinted at it. "Fessenden and someone I guess is our alchemist friend. But what's that behind them? It looks like a goddamn roller coaster."

Nodding, Neuland smiled. "It is. And a Ferris wheel. Look at the name on the side."

Ford picked up the magnifying glass. "*Shangri-La.* Shangri-La at the Beach."

"You're both too young to remember, but I'm not. Back in the thirties it was a huge attraction rivalling Coney Island. But it was largely destroyed in a storm around '39."

"If the place is gone, how does that help us?" said Tilda.

"Look at the small building in the lower right-hand corner. What do you see?"

She took the magnifying glass from Ford and studied the image. "Oh shit," she said.

"Exactly."

"What is it?" said Ford. Tilda handed the magnifying glass back to him. He looked and said, "*Dr. Bacri's House of Wonders and Oddities*. The fucker had a magic show."

"That's great," said Tilda. "But how does it help us that he worked at the beach all those years ago?"

"Because," Neuland went to a laptop set up on a small desk in the corner of the room and pointed to a map on the screen, "after the storm, the city only took away the above-ground wreckage. They paved over the rest. But Dr. Bacri's House of Wonders had an underground wax museum."

Vega came in and stood in the doorway. "And you think he's down there all these years later?"

"For the moment," said Neuland. "I suspect he's been using it on and off over the decades as a refuge when he lost his favored workspace or when the police got too close. Even if there were rumors of a madman down there, who's going to dig up a demolished amusement park?"

"If it's underground, how do we get there?" said Tilda.

"At first I thought we'd have to go through the sewers."

"Eww."

"Agreed. But there's good news. Looking at some of the other details of the photo, I think we can get to the remains with some light B and E."

"B and E?"

"Breaking and entering," said Ford. "To hell with everything else. Let's grab our tools and go get the fucker."

Tilda turned and pointed at him. "Hell no. You were just shot and everybody is exhausted. Between Fessenden getting here and working in the lab, I don't even know if it's day or night anymore, and probably neither do you. There are things I want to do before we go. Plus, we've been drinking. Right now we'll rest, study maps, and go after dark when people are refreshed," she said. "Understand?"

"Yes, ma'am," said Ford.

"Damn right."

"What about the body?" said Vega.

"Neuland is preserving it, so fuck the body," Tilda said. "He's not going anywhere. Let's get some food. I'm starving."

They went back into the living room and Neuland closed the door to the lab. Ford tried making sandwiches, but with his injury Tilda shooed him back to the sofa. He grimaced as he rubbed his arm and said, "Fuck this case."

Pouring some whiskey into a glass, Vega mumbled, "Fuck my life."

17

The alchemist stood in the near dark, mixing a potion by candlelight. He wore a ragged silk robe decorated with sinuous Chinese dragons woven with a real pearl in each beast's mouth. It was a treasured gift from a diplomat he'd loved briefly in Hong Kong a century earlier. But as much as the alchemist had cared for the elegant man, the hunger was more powerful and, in the end, more important.

When he was satisfied with the color of the mixture in the flask he glanced at his watch. Fessenden was late. It was becoming a habit ever since he'd begun gifting the man with bits of his vitality. He wondered if the detective was trying to rise above his station. Perhaps he even had the notion he could steal the secrets of immortality. The alchemist gave the flask another swirl and made a sour face. Going out to the display floor of his dead museum, he backhanded a rat off a wax figure of Marie Antoinette.

Again, he played the memory game, drifting back as far as he could recall. Had he actually known any of the motley celebrities that filled the museum? Had he ever wanted to? Not Vlad Tepes, who always sounded to him like a murderous child. None of the European kings or queens. They all seemed like bores. Even great Ramses in the desert so long ago fell short.

If only he could have made a museum to the truly fascinating figures he'd met over his many years. The ones who deserved commemoration. The killers. The madmen. The mages and salt hags he'd known. The seafarers he'd devoured during long ocean crossings on clipper ships and galleons. Some of them told wonderful stories before he consumed them. There were dying soldiers during a hundred wars—mostly officers because their upper-class flesh tasted sweetest. Actors and dancers in Berlin. A Balinese shaman and a painter in Chicago who'd produced perfect Cézanne forgeries. All these people deserved a museum more than paltry monarchs like Napoleon or Queen Victoria—yet they were what Shangri-La's patrons had demanded. At least he'd been able to provide his unfortunate customers a brief glimpse of other worlds before he fed on them.

As he used his thumb to scrape away mold on Peter the Great's cheek, the alchemist wondered whether Fessenden was worth keeping around even if he did bring the codex. The man knew too much and stank of greed. He'd certainly make an ample meal. The alchemist looked at his watch again, deciding to wait and see what the detective brought him.

18

Before they left the Bunker, Neuland injected Ford with several potions to heal his arm and restore his strength. Then they gathered up their tools into three backpacks and locked Vega downstairs in the gun range.

"It's for your own good," said Neuland. "With our wards, the Bunker is virtually impossible to break into, and the steel door to the range is even harder."

"You'll be safe there," said Tilda in an encouraging tone.

Vega stood on the stairs nervously. "But what if something happens and you don't come back?"

"We're coming back," said Ford.

"Yes, but what if you don't?"

"There's three of us against one. We're coming back."

"I'd feel a lot better if I hadn't seen him kick your asses all over my apartment."

"That was before," said Tilda. "We know a lot more about Bacri now. Especially his weaknesses."

"Please," said Vega.

"Trust me. It's for your own good."

"Did you ever shoot a gun?" said Neuland.

"Once. Amanda took a bunch of us to a range in New Jersey," Vega said.

Ford went to the gun cabinet and retrieved a Desert Eagle .50 caliber pistol. Handing the gun to Vega he said, "That will stop a grizzly bear coming at you on a freight train."

Staring again down into the range Vega finally said, "Okay, I guess. But please don't forget me. Everyone seems to forget about me."

Tilda squeezed his hand. "It's going to be all right. No one is forgetting you and no one is getting to you but us. Trust me."

Vega pressed the pistol to his chest and started down the stairs. Before he reached the bottom Ford yelled down to him, "And for fuck's sake, don't shoot any of us."

"How will I know it's you?"

"I'll wear a white taffeta dress and a gardenia in my hair," said Ford, locking the gun range door.

Tilda shook her head. "Poor Andy. I hope he doesn't hurt himself."

"He'll be fine. The gun isn't loaded."

"Still."

Neuland said, "The best way to keep him safe is to finish the job and get back to him as quickly as possible."

They went out and walked two blocks to the subway where they caught a ride to Queens. It was late enough that they found seats together at the far end of the train car. Setting down their heavy, tool-laden backpacks, Neuland said, "I've been doing some research on groons."

"I don't even want to think about those things," said Tilda. "But I want to hear what you've learned."

"There's only one way to turn a revenant into the kind of murderous groon we saw the other night. It's a substance called black galena. It's very rare. I'm not sure how someone would even find it here. The only nearby sources I know of are Mexico and Molokai, and neither place gives up its galena easily. It's too dangerous. And precious."

"Maybe it was stolen or smuggled?" said Tilda.

"Who would take that chance?" said Ford. "Those outfits in Mexico and Hawaii don't mess around."

Neuland looked down the car at the few other passengers. "It would take a lot of pull or a lot of luck, and I don't believe in that kind of luck."

They got off the subway when it reached the Fort Totten Park stop in Bayside. Hefting their packs onto their shoulders, they went upstairs and out into the cool evening.

The park lay fifty yards ahead of them, illuminated in wan yellowish light from LED lamps. Fog swept around the parkland and smothered the gates in gray trails like vaporous snakes.

"The fog is good luck," said Ford. "It will fuck up their cheap-ass video surveillance."

"How do you know it's cheap?" said Tilda.

"Because New York runs it," Neuland said. "Besides, we're not going to the park. We're looking for a storage building out by the water."

Pointing into the distance Tilda said, "That one?"

Neuland consulted the map he'd printed and his GPS reader. He said, "That's it."

"Great," said Ford. "Let's get going. I'm tired of humping this gear around."

Tilda shifted her pack so it was more comfortable. "Is your shoulder hurting?"

"Nah. I'm just lazy. It's why I hate leaving Manhattan for

the boonies. Too much open space. Too much grass. Too much walking to nothing."

"Ford was born in the subway and raised in an after-hours speakeasy," Neuland said.

"Is that true?" said Tilda.

"One hundred percent," he replied. "I suckled on Jim Beam and learned to make a dark and stormy before I could walk."

"You remember I can tell when you're lying, right?"

"It's all true. I learned to read from the graffiti in the bathroom and to count by shortchanging drunks."

"I bet all the girls liked you when you were little."

"When they weren't breaking my heart. Never fall in love with goth girls from the Limelight when you're six."

"I'll remember that."

Finally, they reached a chain-link fence around a large storage building on the edge of the bay. The breeze off the water chilled the night, but the air smelled fresh. Tilda took in deep lungfuls.

Ford set down his backpack, took out a large set of bolt cutters and quickly snipped through the chain holding the front gate closed. They went inside and sprinted to the building.

Tilda tried the door, but it was locked. She turned to Neuland. "Can you use the thing you used to open the lock to Goss's apartment building?"

"No," he said. "This lock is too old and rusted from the salt air."

"Are we going to pick it?"

Neuland took a small sledgehammer from his pack and slammed it down on the doorknob twice. With the second blow, the entire lock mechanism fell out and they went inside. Checking his map again, Neuland led them down to the basement.

"You're up next, T," said Ford.

Tilda set down her backpack and pulled out an electric reciprocating saw. She was nervous. She'd never used a saw like this but had volunteered eagerly when they were dividing up jobs. "Which wall are we going through?" she said.

Neuland studied his map for a moment and pointed off to her left. "That one."

Tilda approached a solid wall constructed from heavy wooden panels and looked it over. "How do I get started? There's nowhere for the saw blade to go."

"Leave it to me," said Ford. He took a small chainsaw from his bag and set to work cutting into the wall. The saw was loud and kicked wood chips in all directions. It took several minutes of Ford working on the wood, gouging the twelve-inch blade deeper and deeper into the wall. Finally, the saw slipped inside the wall up to the trigger. Ford wiped a sleeve across his sweaty brow.

"I'm all the way through," he said. "It's up to you now."

Tilda inserted the blade of her saw into the hole Ford had created and turned on the machine. It almost jumped out of her hand at first, but she leaned into it, using her weight and the strength in her shoulders to cut two long lines down the wood, then then a horizontal line linking them. When she was done, she tried kicking at the wall to move it from the opening she'd created.

"Ow. Fuck," she shouted, hopping on one foot.

Neuland and Ford came up and stood on either side of her. "Let's try it together," said Neuland. "On three. One. Two—"

On "three" they kicked the panel all at once, and after two more kicks it fell back into darkness with a loud *crack*. Stale air drifted into the room, mixed with the smell of tidal rot and brine. Tilda put the saw back in her bag and peered into the darkness. "We're really going in there, huh," she said.

"The first assholes in almost a century," Ford said.

"Who goes first?"

"Flip for it?"

They each took a quarter from their pocket, flipped it into the air and caught it.

Looking at Ford and Neuland's quarters—which both showed heads—Tilda quietly said, "Shit."

Ford handed her a flashlight and said, "Remember how scared you were of everything when we first met you?"

"Yeah. I used to jump at my own shadow."

"Look at you now, killer. You can do this."

"I can," Tilda said. "Let's go."

19

Tilda stepped through the hole into near total darkness and slowly moved her flashlight over the space. Technically she could still see in the dark, but the sensation unnerved her, so she was happy to use the light.

Every inch of the walls and bare floor was covered in mildew and dust. She had to blink a couple of times to clear her vision. When she did, the first thing she saw was a large canvas sign covered in a lurid painting of a snake wrapped around a nude woman, with the reptile's head sitting where the woman's head should be. Florid red letters above the painting read *Madame Caramella, the Snake Woman*. Below the canvas was a crumbling frame where a door once stood.

Next to that was what looked like the remains of an old shooting gallery. A few ragged Kewpie dolls, their faces and bodies mostly obscured under a thick coating of gray mold, stood on racks waiting for the amusement park sharp shooters who'd never come.

"Everything okay in there?" said Ford.

Tilda replied, "Everything is fine. Weird, but fine. Come in. I think I found one of your crushes, Ford."

He and Neuland stepped through the opening, their own flashlights illuminating the way. There were ring toss games and a kissing booth with a painting of a bearded lady. Tilda pointed to Madame Caramella and said, "One of your goth girls?"

Ford put his hand on his chest and said, "Bestill my heart." Then, "It looks like there's a whole street of old attractions. How are we going to find the museum?"

"From the map, it looks like this area is largely a straight shot from end to end," Neuland said. "There might be some turn-offs, but my guess is that the museum will be on the main walkway."

"Do your funny eyes see anything interesting, T?" said Ford.

"Nothing unusual so far."

"Cool. Let's get going."

"Wait," Neuland said. "Remember, when we get there, Bacri is mine."

Ford frowned. "Come on, man. This isn't some ordinary asshole we're chasing."

Neuland looked down into the dark. "You kill the dead. I kill the living. And Bacri is very much alive."

"Okay. But if things go sideways I'm not letting that piece of shit take you down over a job description."

Turning to them both, Neuland said, "Remember that he's afraid of people like me. That should give me an advantage."

"Maybe," said Tilda. "But I'm with Ford. No one dies tonight but him."

"How are you going for him?" Ford said.

Neuland reached into his jacket and brought out a karambit with a six-inch crescent-moon-shaped blade. "Guns don't seem to stop him, so I brought this. Let's see how well he fights when he's gutted and holding on to his intestines."

Tilda said, "Just be careful. I haven't finished reading the codex. He might have spells or wards that we don't know about."

"Noted. Let's get moving."

As quietly as they could, they moved down the walkway, their flashlights revealing the tumbledown remains of food stands and ancient freak shows. When they came to a crossroads, Ford went a short distance down one while Tilda walked down the other. Each came back shaking their heads.

"Nothing," said Tilda.

Neuland studied the map as they went. They walked for several minutes more when he held up a hand for the others to stop. He said, "Smell that? Something sweet. Like perfume or cologne. The museum should be just a few yards ahead. Whatever happens, I'm going in first and you two are backup. Understood?"

"Understood," said Tilda. Ford nodded.

A little farther on, Neuland stopped them again. He turned off his flashlight and said, "Up there. It looks like candlelight."

The others turned off their flashlights. A few yards ahead a dim buttery light flickered. Without another word, Neuland put away the map and brought up the karambit. Holding out an arm to keep the others back, he advanced toward the museum.

It wasn't long before they saw it: a wide, cracked wooden sign on which gold and blue lettering proclaimed *The Gallery of Historical Curiosities*. There was no door, just a threadbare curtain hanging over the entrance. Neuland pushed through it slowly, leaving the others outside.

Inside the museum, he found himself in a large room flanked by dozens of wax figures on pedestals behind purple velvet ropes. Their glass eyes seem to burn in the light from dozens of candles lit throughout the place. Between the exhibits were piles of discarded human bones. More hung from hooks in the ceiling, some with shreds of decomposing flesh left on.

Trophies, he thought.

Neuland advanced cautiously, gazing into the shadows, waiting for an ambush. But nothing happened. He made his way through the main room down a smaller corridor along a long row of dusty royalty. The museum was dead quiet. There was a brighter light up ahead, so he moved in that direction. Until his boot crunched down on a broken femur. It sounded like a gunshot in the near silence of the place. Curtains a few yards in the distance wavered.

"Fessenden," came a deep voice. "You're late again." Then the curtains parted and there he was, dressed in his elegant, filthy robe.

Neuland and Bacri stared at each other for a long moment. "You're not Fessenden," said the alchemist. Eventually, a smile creeped across his face. "I remember you," he said. "You were in the little man's apartment. You didn't happen to bring my book with you, by any chance?"

"No, but I have it. I'll even tell you where it is. But only if I can whisper it to you."

Bacri took a few steps in Neuland's direction, looking him over. "I like your choice of weapons. Nothing as boorish as a gun. It's something old. Something with a bit of character."

Neuland, who'd been in a fighting stance, relaxed his body and stood up straight, putting his hands behind his back. "If you want your book come closer. We both know you're faster than I am. From this position, I can't possibly hurt you."

Bacri looked at him warily. "I wonder if that's true," he said blurring as he rushed at Neuland in a fraction of a second. The alchemist grabbed Neuland's jacket and lifted him a few inches off the ground. "Now," he said. "Whisper to me."

Neuland leaned down to him, close enough that their cheeks almost touched.

Bacri gasped and drew in a ragged breath. The whites of his eyes flooded with blood and he stumbled back with a racking cough, shoving Neuland away.

"So, you don't like my kind after all," he said, swinging the karambit at Bacri's throat. The alchemist twisted away and, still coughing, kicked Neuland in the midsection, sending him onto his back. Then Bacri was standing over him, red streaks running from his eyes like tears, raising up a heel to crush Neuland's skull. He swung the karambit, cutting a long slit in the alchemist's thigh. Bacri screamed and stumbled away as red cascaded from his severed femoral artery.

The alchemist stumbled into a wax figure of Ivan the Terrible, knocking it to the floor and shattering its head into a hundred pieces. Before Neuland could close in on him, Bacri grabbed the golden staff the czar had been holding and hit Neuland on the side of his head. While Neuland was dizzy from the blow, Bacri hobbled to the back of the museum and disappeared behind a curtain. Neuland went after him and ripped the curtain from its rod, throwing open the alchemist's workspace. A flask crashed against Neuland's head and a noxious potion ran into his eyes, blinding him for a moment. More flasks came flying and broke against him. Unable to see, Neuland had to fall back. While he was helpless, Bacri stumbled past him out into the museum.

Where he ran right into Tilda and Ford, who was drawing a sawed-off shotgun from his pack. But even injured, Bacri was fast. He knocked Tilda to the floor and slapped the shotgun from Ford's hands. Before he could react, the blood-soaked alchemist grabbed Ford's wrists and squeezed.

Ford let out a wail and tried to pull away, but already the skin on his hands was softening. Bacri squeezed harder as the need to feed and heal his injury overwhelmed everything else.

Ford fell to his knees as Tilda got into a kneeling position and shot Bacri twice in the side. Falling back a few steps, he released Ford and rushed at her. She shot him twice more and the alchemist fell, a shocked look on his face as he vomited thick blood streaked with black.

Neuland stumbled out of the back of the museum. Ford watched as Tilda pulled a Bowie knife from her jacket and kicked Bacri over. Using all her weight, Tilda dropped down onto her knees, driving the knife into the base of the alchemist's skull. Bacri screamed once and reached back to grab at Tilda. She raised the heavy knife again and brought it down on his neck, severing his head.

Neuland and Ford came over to them and stared down at the unmoving alchemist.

Ford rubbed at his injured wrists. "Exactly what the fuck did you just do?"

Breathing hard, Tilda drew herself to her feet. She kicked Bacri once and said, "I hope you don't mind. Remember when I said I had something to do last night? Well, I went into the lab and put some of Neuland's blood on my bullets and knife. I probably should have said something, but—"

Ford grabbed her in a hug and said, "You're my fucking genius hero."

Neuland said, "He's right. Bacri might have won without you."

When Ford released her from the hug Tilda kicked Bacri again and said, "You hear that, old man? We beat you."

"Is he dead?" said Ford.

Tilda shook her head. “No. After all these centuries he’s still strong enough that, from what I read in the codex, I don’t think we can ever kill him completely. But there’s something we can do to stop him.”

“Show us,” said Neuland.

Tilda went back to her pack and took out the reciprocating saw. “We take him apart,” she said. “We take him apart and never let the pieces get close to each other again.”

Ford took the chainsaw from his pack. “Sounds good to me.”

“Is it really that simple?” said Neuland.

Frowning, Tilda said, “I’m afraid not. Ideally, we’d burn each part of him down to ashes and scatter them at separate locations where they can never join again. But there’s no way we can start a fire down here.”

Neuland glanced back at Bacri’s workspace. “Could we dissolve him? Reduce him to liquid and put him into vessels?”

“That might be all right,” Tilda said.

“I have an idea what to do with him,” said Ford. He fired up his chainsaw. “But let’s have some fun first.”

Neuland went to Bacri’s potions as Tilda and Ford sawed the alchemist into a dozen bloody pieces. When they were done, Neuland came back with two jars containing a clear fluid. “I found some oil of alkahest. We can take Bacri back to the Bunker, dissolve him, and dispose of the remains safely.”

The three of them loaded the body parts into their packs and made their way out of the storage building back to the subway. Filthy and exhausted, Ford took out a flask of whiskey, which he and Tilda passed back and forth. Neuland toasted them with goofer juice as they relaxed at the end of the car.

A few minutes before they reached their stop, Neuland touched his forehead. Dark webbing outlined the veins and arteries of his face and throat, coursing down his arms so that his fingertips turned a deep blue-black. He managed to stumble out of the car but collapsed on the subway platform.

Tilda and Ford had to carry him the last few blocks to the Bunker.

20

They dragged Neuland into his lab and hoisted him onto an old medical exam table.

Ford shouted, "What the hell is happening to him?"

Tilda lifted Neuland's eyelids and found his pupils had expanded so much that his eyes seemed almost entirely black. "I'm not completely sure," she said. "But I think one of the potions Bacri threw at him must have been something that attacks revenants."

"What can we do about it?"

"I might find something in the codex, but it will take time."

"Get on it. I'll stay with him."

Shaking her head, Tilda said, "Look at his hands. They're completely dark now. Whatever the potion was, the effect is spreading."

Ford said, "Please don't let him die. You know, really die."

Tilda thought for a moment. "I have an idea that might stabilize him for a little while. But it might make things worse."

"We're already losing him. Try it."

She took a breath and said, "Okay. Here goes."

Taking a pair of snippers, Tilda went to Fessenden's preserved corpse and cut off his thumb. Dropping it into a laboratory blender, she hit the on button. It took a minute, but the spinners finally rendered the flesh and bone into a milky liquid.

"What the hell is that?" said Ford.

"Bacri gave Fessenden some of his strength. I'm hoping we can transfer a little of that power into Neuland."

"Hurry. Please."

Tilda unstopped a bottle of goofer juice and poured it into the blender until the finger mixture was thin enough that she could draw it into a syringe. The first shot she injected into the right side of Neuland's throat, then the left. She ripped open his shirt and was shocked to find most of his veins and capillaries outlined in the same blue-black pattern as his throat and hands.

"What happens now?" said Ford.

Tilda put the syringe into a tray. "I'm hoping this will slow Bacri's potion long enough for me to figure this out. Or maybe I'm just wasting time. I don't know."

She and Ford watched as the darkness slowly crept across Neuland's body. Tilda said, "If the infection reaches his throat, it might be too late."

Going around the table, Tilda stood with Ford. Inch by inch, Neuland's veins and capillaries became visible as they filled with poison.

"God," she said quietly. "I don't think—"

"There!" shouted Ford. He pointed to Neuland's collar bone. "I think it's slowing."

Tilda stared at the veins on Neuland's chest, waiting to see if the infection would move upward. But the creeping darkness seemed to stop in place. "You're right," she said. "I think it might have worked."

"You should get back to the codex," said Ford. "I'm going to stay here and keep an eye on him."

"Let me know if anything changes," said Tilda, but Ford didn't reply.

In the living room, she opened the codex to the last section she'd been reading, one that seemed to describe the first complex methods of imbuing a body with immortality. The Latin in that section grew maddeningly convoluted. She frequently had to consult a dictionary.

From somewhere, she heard a frantic banging. Then came a voice, "Hello! Is anyone out there?"

Recognizing Vega's cries, Tilda opened the gun range door and found him on the stairs panting and sweating. He jabbed a finger at her. "I knew you people would forget about me. I knew it," he shouted.

"Calm down, Andy," Tilda said. "Things have been crazy. Neuland is dying."

She went to the sofa and Vega followed her over. He said, "I thought he was dead."

"He is. But if we don't do something he's going to be *dead* dead."

"I don't—"

"Please," she said. "Get yourself a drink or make some coffee or something but let me work."

He headed into the kitchen and said, "I'm sorry about your friend."

"Shh."

Tilda read for another hour, poring over obscure methods and formulae until her eyes burned. While the text was mostly in Latin, the illustrations looked like something clipped from books in ancient Egyptian. There were animal-headed gods, symbols for rivers, and the sun. Little of it made sense to her until she came to a section about travel to the Western Lands and the Egyptian afterlife. Finally, one glittering illustration below an image of Osiris caught her eye and she shouted, "Ford!"

He came running into the living room, looking scared. "What is it? You okay?"

Tilda grinned and held up the book. "I think I might have found it."

Ford sat down next to her. She ran her finger along the Latin text to a section describing the goddess of resurrection. "If I'm reading this right, the trick to immortality is to die and then be brought back to life with a secret potion. The most secret potion ever."

"Does it say what it is?"

"It does. The section is complicated, but it goes step by step along the way."

"So, what do you need?" Ford said.

"Neuland already has a lot of the ingredients and the rest are fairly commonplace. There's only one I'm not sure about."

"What's that?"

"A powder made from a jewel scarab beetle. A gold one is best."

Ford fell back against the sofa. "Do you know how rare jewel scarab beetles are around here? Especially gold ones?"

"They're absolutely essential for the resurrection potion."

"Goddammit," said Ford. "There's only place in town that might possibly have it, but I don't know if we can even get in."

Tilda set down the book. "Where are you thinking?"

"Mama Kelvina. She's the only potion maker in New York who might have some. And she doesn't like Neuland or me."

"Who would she talk to?"

Ford went into the kitchen where Vega was drinking coffee.

He smiled at the nervous man. "Vega," said Ford. "Andy. You're tight with Amanda Goss, aren't you?"

Vega shrugged. "We're friends."

"Do you have her phone number?"

"Of course."

"Call her."

Looking at his watch, Vega said, "It's the middle of the night."

"Amanda's a late night gal. Call her. If she gets mad tell her you'll make it up to her."

"What am I supposed to say?"

"You're going to have Amanda call Mama Kelvina and tell her that she's the one who wants the jewel scarab powder."

"She's going to ask why."

"Tell her if she wants the Skinner caught she'll do it."

Vega looked at him. "I thought you were going out to kill him. Oh shit. Is he still alive and looking for me?"

"Relax. The Skinner is dead. But no one knows it but us. You're going to get Amanda to call Mama Kelvina for the powder."

"Is that all?"

Ford shook his head. "There's one more thing."

"What? I don't want to get killed after all this."

"Relax. All you have to do is go to Mama Kelvina's, pick up the powder, and bring it back here."

Vega set down his coffee cup, looking uncomfortable. "Why me?"

From the sofa, Tilda said, "Because you're the richest man we know."

Ford nodded. "That's right. You're going because you can pay Mama any fucked-up, middle-of-the-night, crazy-ass amount of money she wants."

Vega shook his head. "I don't want to go. I won't do it."

"Andy," said Ford, an edge in his voice.

Tilda came over and gently pushed Ford out of the way. She led Vega to a chair and pulled him down as she sat too. "Listen. Remember how you told us that no one ever took you seriously or invited you to their parties?"

"You don't have to rub it in."

"This is your chance to be remembered. For all anyone else knows, Bacri is still alive and wandering the streets. But you, Andy, you can be part of the team that brings him down. You'll be a hero. You'll get more party invitations than you could possibly attend. No one will ever forget you," Tilda said. "What do you say? Are you ready to be the most popular man in New York?"

Vega looked down. He picked a speck of something off his pants and put his hands together. Then he looked at Tilda and said, "No."

"Andy!" she shouted. "Do you remember? We saved you from Fessenden."

"Yes, I remember. And I'm paying you a lot of money for it."

Ford said, "Keep it."

Tilda and Vega looked at him.

"Keep the money," said Ford. "Keep your money and do us one favor for saving your ass." He put a hand up to his shoulder and winced.

"What's wrong?" said Tilda.

"Nothing."

She went to him and pushed back his jacket. "You're bleeding again. You must have ripped out your stitches. We need to take care of this before you lose too much blood."

"I'm fine."

Tilda turned to Vega and said, "Ford got shot protecting you from Fessenden. Neuland is dying because Bacri poisoned him after we all stopped him from killing you. But sit there, Andy. Sit there and do nothing because that's all you are. Nothing. Come on, Ford." She led him from the from the room back into the lab. Once there she said, "I don't know how to do the stitches like Neuland. But I can pack the wound and get you to the hospital."

"No way," he said. "I'm not leaving."

"But you need someone who can close the wound for good."

Ford sat down on a lab stool and said, "Listen to me, T. Neuland is my friend. He's also my partner in this fucked-up little outfit we have here. And the first rule is, you don't leave your partner behind. Period."

Tilda got a first aid kit and took out some gauze. She said, "Okay. If you're not going anywhere neither am I. We stick together no matter what."

"No matter what."

A few moments later, as Tilda used medical tape to secure gauze to Ford's shoulder, Vega stood in the lab doorway. "Knock knock," he said.

Tilda kept working on Ford and didn't look up. "What do you want, Andy?"

He sighed. "I called Amanda."

"Oh?"

"Man was she pissed. But she's going to call that Mama Kelvina person. I'm waiting for her to call me back."

When Tilda finished working on Ford, she went over and gave Vega a quick hug.

"Thanks. I know that was hard."

Vega looked at the floor. "I was scared. But I'm getting pretty used to that."

Ford said, "You're going to have a lot fewer reasons to be scared after this."

"That would be nice."

Vega's phone rang a few minutes later. When he hung up he said, "Everything is ready."

Ford wrote out Mama Kelvina's address and gave it to Vega. He called a car service and left soon after.

When Vega was gone, Ford put a hand on Neuland's head and said, "You pain in the ass."

Tilda kissed Ford on the cheek and they sat together in silence.

21

Ford cursed as he checked his watch every few minutes, to the point that Tilda put her hand over his to make him stop looking. The silence and the waiting went on. Neuland lay on the table, full of poison, and the two of them stared, looking for any sign that the infection was spreading or subsiding. Nothing changed. Tilda brought over lab stools so they could sit, but Ford refused at first. Finally, she said, "I slowed the bleeding, but you're still hurt. Neuland wouldn't want you making things worse for yourself." Ford looked away at first, but a moment later sat down.

It was an hour before the front door buzzer went off. Tilda rushed into the living room to let Vega in. He was carrying a large brown paper bag.

Ford came out from the lab. "What took so long?" he said.

Vega handed the bag to Tilda and said, "That Mama woman wasn't exactly happy to see me. She kept asking a lot of questions about what all that stuff was for."

"What did you tell her?" said Tilda.

"That I was doing a favor for Amanda."

Ford headed back into the lab with Tilda. "Good enough. You got everything?"

"I think so. I hope so. It cost enough."

Tilda spread out the ingredients and began mixing the potion. It went slowly since she had to consult the codex at each step.

"How can I help?" said Ford.

She handed him a pile of glittering carapaces. "These are the scarabs. Grind them to a powder with that mortar and pestle."

"On it."

As they worked, Vega stood by Neuland staring at his blackened body. After a few minutes he said, "Hey, you guys. Is this supposed to be happening? That black stuff is moving around on his chest."

While Tilda worked, Ford said, "Hurry up, T. The poison is spreading again."

She poured the powdered scarabs into the brew she was heating up and stirred it until it turned metallic and opaque, like golden mercury. "Almost there," she said. A moment later she yelled "Fuck!"

"What is it?" said Ford.

"It says that the last ingredient is the marrow of the living."

Ford and Tilda looked at Vega. He held up his hands and said, "That's everything she gave me, I swear."

Tilda set the potion down. "I don't know what to do. I don't know what to do. Fuck."

Ford shoved Vega out of the way and went around Neuland's body. By Fessenden's corpse, he picked up the snippers that Tilda had used earlier. Slamming his hand down on the lab table, he slipped the first joint of his pinky finger between the blades. "Shit," he said quietly.

And cut off his finger.

"Ford!" Tilda shouted.

He managed to hand it to Tilda before slumping to the floor saying, "Sorry. I—I need to sit down."

She took a scalpel and gouged the bone from the joint and yelled at Vega. "Help him, Andy. Get some gauze and put pressure on his finger to stop the bleeding."

With the scalpel, Tilda scooped as much marrow out of the finger as she could and added it to the golden potion. After mixing everything, she drew some into a large syringe and went to Neuland.

"Get me on my feet, Vega," said Ford. "I need to be there for this."

Ford staggered up as Tilda poised with the syringe over Neuland's heart.

"What if I did it wrong?" she said. "I might kill him."

"No, you won't," said Ford. "You're going to save his ass, and then mine."

"I'm so sorry, Neuland."

"Do it!"

Tilda slammed the syringe down with a crack as it passed between his ribs and into Neuland's heart.

The dark traceries crept up his body, inky tendrils from his chest touching those moving down from his throat. He was almost completely engulfed in Bacri's poison. No one spoke. Tilda went over and held Ford's good hand. He slumped against her. With a small shudder, Ford's legs gave out and he almost fell back to the floor. Vega caught him and maneuvered him onto a lab stool.

Tilda checked Ford's mangled finger. "Now we really need to get you a hospital."

"No," he said. "You can fix me up."

"I can't. I couldn't even save—" Her voice trailed off and she put her arms around Ford. "I'm sorry." She began to cry and Ford put an arm around her.

From behind them Vega said, "Hey. Is this supposed to be happening?" Tilda turned to where he was pointing. "That black stuff. It's doing something weird. Like bubbling."

Tilda gently moved Vega out of the way and wiped at the substance—like sticky, thickened blood—oozing up from Neuland's chest. When she drew the sponge away, the skin looked clear. As they watched, the poison drained in a bubbling trickle from Neuland's body, flowing like black sludge across the table and onto the floor. As Tilda stepped away from the body Ford said, "You did it. You fucking did it."

It took several minutes, but Neuland's body slowly seemed to shrug off the last of the poison. But he still didn't move.

Ford stood by him, "Come on, fucker."

Tilda pushed Neuland's eyelids open. "His pupils. They reacted to light," she said.

"That's good, right? He's—"

Neuland's whole body spasmed in a deep, racking cough. He rocked from side to side, sliding in the black muck on the table. Tilda and Ford had to grab him so he wouldn't fall off. Finally, they sat him upright on the table. Neuland's head lolled back as he continued to cough, which in a couple of minutes turned into a deep rasping breath. Then another. Neuland's eyes opened. Ford and Tilda held him up and he grabbed their arms.

Speaking in a low, choking voice, Neuland said, "I can breathe."

"How is it, man?" said Ford.

He shook his head and coughed again. "I don't—It's been a hundred years. It hurts."

"Andy. Get him a blanket from one of the chairs," said Tilda as she wiped the last of the poison off Neuland with a towel.

The three of them walked him haltingly into the living room and set him down on the sofa. He looked at Ford and Tilda. "What did you do to me?" he said.

She said, "We used Bacri's alchemy and brought you back."

Neuland raised a hand in Ford's direction. "What's wrong with you? You look like a ghost."

Ford waved off the remark. "I'm just a little tired."

"He's lost a lot of blood," said Tilda. "And part of a finger. But he won't let me take him to a hospital."

Neuland sat up a little straighter. "Get my surgery kit. I'll talk you through how to stitch him up."

When she'd stopped the bleeding in Ford's finger and shoulder, both he and Neuland fell into a deep sleep where they were. Tilda poured whiskey for Vega and herself and sat nearby watching the two men breathe.

Sometime later, Ford raised his head. "It's time, T."

"Time for what?" she said.

"Tomorrow we call the other outfits and get them back over here. Tell them we took care of the Skinner."

"Will you be in shape for that?"

"Hell yes." He smiled. "And I have an idea I want to run by you. Something I thought of while you were working on Neuland."

"Tell me," she said, but he'd fallen back to sleep.

22

During the night, Neuland became more used to breathing and put his bottles of goofer juice away. In the morning he ate a few bites of toast and drank half a cup of coffee with the others. They changed Ford's bandages and put his arm in a sling. Tilda changed into jeans and slipped a 9mm pistol into a holster behind her back. Vega didn't touch his toast or coffee.

"Why can't I go home?" he said.

Ford adjusted his sling. "Just because we killed some people doesn't mean this is over. It's not safe for you yet."

"Why? The Skinner and Fessenden are dead. You got everybody."

"Did we?" said Neuland.

"How are you, T?" said Ford.

"Ready to go."

Vega retreated downstairs to the gun range.

An hour later, the heads of the six outfits that had come to Ford and Neuland with the Skinner job were back in their living room.

Eddie Jourgensen nodded at Ford's bandages. "It looks like you got hit by a truck."

"I did. But the truck is dead, so I guess we're even."

Amanda Goss went over and stood very close to Neuland. "Are you—are you breathing?"

He took in a deep breath and let it out. "You tell me."

"Damn you. You're alive. You figured it out, didn't you? Immortality. You made a deal with the Skinner."

"The Skinner is dead," said Ford.

Mendez said, "Where's the body?"

Tilda brought out six old brown glass jars from the kitchen and handed one to each of the outfit heads. "I wouldn't open those if I were you. They're not exactly perfume."

"What you're holding in your hands," said Neuland, "are the remains of the Skinner. We fought him and beat him. But he can't ever be fully killed. So, we rendered his body useless and now present him to you."

Ford said, "You fuckers all acted together when you dropped this problem on us. Fine. You're all responsible now. Pour your piece in the Atlantic. Drop it in a volcano. Put it under your bed. The point is if we—and I mean all of us—keep him in pieces, and apart, he'll be helpless forever."

"It's your responsibility to deal with your piece," said Neuland. "If anyone loses theirs or cheats, Tilda will be able to tell."

Jourgensen held up his jar. "You already lost some of him. Mine's empty."

"About that," said Tilda. "The only reason any of this was able to happen is because one of you was working with Fessenden and the Skinner."

Neuland said, "That person arranged for the groon to go after

Vega, hoping it would kill him and implicate us. Or, if he got lucky, it would kill all of us so the police could say we were the Skinner. This person never wanted the Skinner stopped because they wanted the same thing as Fessenden—immortality."

"Fessenden was just a front man for someone who protected the Skinner until they could get his secret from him," said Ford. "But what's immortality worth if you're broke? Whoever was working with the Skinner promised Fessenden a long life and all the money they could ever want when he delivered the secret."

"Whoever it was should have killed us themselves," said Neuland. "But the groon gave them away. You can only make that kind of vicious groon using black galena. And who here runs those kinds of exotic ingredients?"

Goss and the others looked at Jourgensen. He crossed his arms and said, "I haven't seen galena in years."

Ford said, "So what? When you did have it, you passed some of it on to the only person in New York who would know exactly what to do with it. Mama Kelvina. The witch who'll brew up anything you want. But anything really dangerous? She'll only do that for family."

"You're just looking for excuses for fucking up so badly."

"You didn't answer my question," said Ford. "Who here could have given Mama black galena?"

"I barely speak to the old hag," said Jourgensen.

"He's lying," said Tilda. "How about Fessenden?"

"I don't know him either."

"Another lie."

"How does she know he's lying?" said Ligotti.

Neuland said, "Her special sight. Another gift from the Skinner."

Ford walked to Jourgensen. "Fessenden was your cousin,

wasn't he? Someone you could trust. Someone who'd share immortality with you because you're both Mama's boys."

Jourgensen stepped back and looked at the other outfit heads. "You know this is all bullshit, right?"

Neuland set something down on the coffee table. "This is the handkerchief I used to sample the groon's blood. I've already run my tests and know the truth. It's full of galena. If any of you want to run your own tests, feel free."

Goss snatched up the handkerchief and put it in her pocket. "What do you have to say for yourself, Jourgensen?"

"First off, fuck you, Amanda. You trust these assholes? They have the immortality formula. Now they're just trying to get us to fight among ourselves."

Ford said, "Which one of you wants a groon on your doorstep when Jourgensen decides to take your territory? Or maybe he'll send it for your family. Blackmail you for what he wants."

Jourgensen pulled a small Derringer from his jacket sleeve and pointed it at Ford. Tilda pulled her pistol, but Jourgensen howled and grabbed his arm. A knife protruded from it. Goss pulled another knife but didn't bother throwing it as Mendez and the heads of the other outfits grabbed Jourgensen and pinned him to the floor.

"I don't care what you do with him, but don't do it here," said Ford firmly.

Goss twisted her knife in Jourgensen's arm and said, "What about the Skinner's gold?"

"What about it, Jourgensen?" said Neuland. "We didn't find it in his hideout. It's still out there somewhere. Or does it even exist?"

Jourgensen looked around at his captors and shouted, "No, no. It's real! Amanda, I'll tell you where it is."

Goss pulled her knife from his arm. "Oh, you'll tell me all right."

"What about our cut?" said Ford.

Wiping blood from her knife, Goss said, "You get to live and to work again. Be grateful for that."

Ford started to say something, but Neuland put a hand on his shoulder and said, "We are. But no more threats and no more games."

"Of course," said Goss. "But what about what they did to you, Neuland? Aren't you going to share immortality with the rest of us?"

Tilda said, "Neuland isn't immortal. He's just not dead anymore. Besides, you saw what the Skinner had to do all those years to stay alive. We have no interest in seeing a dozen of him running around eating people."

"So, you're keeping the secret for yourselves."

"We're not keeping anything. I burned the codex last night. I'll show you the ashes if you like."

Goss cocked her head at Tilda. "You're just that naive, aren't you? I bet your two friends wanted to keep it."

"Maybe. But they left the decision to me. And now it's gone."

"Pity," said Goss. "I'll be sad to watch that pretty face of yours fall apart. Yours too, Neuland."

"What about my pretty face?" said Ford.

"You're just lucky I believed half of your nonsense today. If I find out you've been lying—"

"I haven't."

"We'll see," she said and gestured to the other outfit heads. "Bring Jourgensen along. We're going to have a party with him. Mama too."

After locking up, Tilda said, "How did you know all that about Jourgensen?"

"It was the only thing that made sense," said Neuland.

"Goss was right," said Ford. "A lot of it was bullshit, but I knew you could tell who was lying if I got even close to the truth."

Vega came up from the gun range with the codex in his hands. "What do you want me to do with this?"

"Just leave it on the table for now, Andy," said Tilda. "We'll figure out what to do with it later."

Neuland said, "You were right before when you said it was best to burn it."

"I know. It's just that working on the codex was the first time I felt like I was doing something only I could do. You know, as part of the team."

"You already bring something unique to the team," said Neuland.

"What's that?"

"You," said Ford "We wouldn't have made it through this mess without you. You don't need Satan's Rolodex to prove yourself."

Tilda picked up the codex and put it on her lap. "Should we burn the thing in the oven or on the roof?"

"On the roof. If there's any spooks living in there I don't want them loose down here."

Vega went to the door. "Is it okay if I leave?"

"It's fine. You're safe now," said Neuland.

"Thanks. I'll do a wire transfer for the money when I get home."

"I told you to keep it," said Ford.

"You ruined my apartment, but you saved my life. I pay my debts."

When Vega was gone, they went to the roof of the Bunker

with the codex and a can of lighter fluid. Neuland poured it all over the book and Tilda sparked a match. They watched the pages burn down to a fine ash, which was carried into the sky on a cool breeze.

23

Tilda took the subway across town and walked the last couple of blocks to Arsenic Green. This time she didn't pause outside but walked right in the door.

Inside, women turned to glance at her as she moved through the place. She liked the coolness of the room. The dim lights. Some of the strange cocktails the revenant women drank shimmered and changed colors, the surface seeming to move on its own.

Toward the back of the bar, in a tufted velvet booth, Tilda found Amanda Goss drinking with a couple of friends. Goss raised an eyebrow at her and said, "Oh look. It's the little pyromaniac. What can we do for you, darling?"

Tilda moved around to the other side of the booth and slid inside so that she was directly across from Goss. "How's your drink?" Tilda said.

"Lovely. But nothing someone like you could handle."

"Do they make regular, you know, human drinks here?"

Goss's lips curled up in a minute smile. "They do indeed. What are you having?"

"A Manhattan."

Goss called over a waitress and made the order for her, then turned her attention back to Tilda. "Now that your drink is on the way, maybe you'll tell me what's going on. Did Neuland or Ford send you?"

"They don't even know I'm here."

"Let you off the leash, did they?"

"No one leashes me without my consent."

Goss's smile quirked up just a little more. "All right then. What are you doing here?"

"Well," Tilda said slowly. "The last time I was here one of your friends mentioned they could show me things that would blow my mind."

"Did they?"

When Tilda's drink arrived she pushed it out of the way and said, "Yes. But I figured why not go to someone who *really* knows things. What do you say, Amanda? Want to blow my mind?"

Now Goss smiled widely and easily, as did Tilda. They drank together until the bar closed and walked arm in arm into the New York night.

ACKNOWLEDGEMENTS

As always, I'd like to thank my wonderful agent, Ginger Clark, without whom I wouldn't have a career. I also want to thank my terrific editor, George Sandison, who helped me pull *The Flesh King* together. Thanks also to my friends Violet, Erica, Jim, and Stefan who helped keep me sane. And, of course, my cat Aces, who is my harshest critic when I won't let him sleep on my shoulder when I'm working.

ABOUT THE AUTHOR

Richard Kadrey is the *New York Times* bestselling author of the Sandman Slim supernatural noir series. *Sandman Slim* was included in Amazon's "100 Science Fiction & Fantasy Books to Read in a Lifetime." Some of Kadrey's other books include *The Pale House Devil*, *Butcher Bird*, and *The Dead Take the A Train* (with Cassandra Khaw). His work has been nominated for the BSFA, Locus, and Dragon awards and appeared in Best Horror of the Year. Aside from books, Kadrey has written for film and comics, including *Heavy Metal*, *Lucifer*, and *Hellblazer*. Kadrey also makes music with his band, A Demon in Fun City.

"Gritty, propulsive, and deliciously pulpy. Richard Kadrey's *The Flesh King* seized my attention on page one and did not release me until the final act. Written with such caustic wittiness and filled with an undeniably sinister atmosphere, this remarkable noir-horror-hybrid is a nasty delight."

Eric LaRocca

"Nobody writes urban supernatural noir like Richard Kadrey! *The Flesh King* is wonderfully nasty business, with a hideous villain and a loveably grumpy and weird found family of hardboiled occult investigators and assassins-for-good. Mean streets, dark magic, grotesque murder... yes, please!"

Christopher Golden

"Fast, fun, and freaky! A delightfully fresh take on horror-noir with a beating heart of solid pulp and characters you'll follow to the gates of hell. I love this series!"

Delilah S. Dawson

"*The Flesh King* leaves you wanting more. That's the point. Kadrey deepens his world, complicates his characters, and serves up a villain nasty enough to justify the whole enterprise. It's fast, bloody, and weirdly warm in ways that shouldn't work but absolutely do."

Ginger Nuts of Horror

"Another good read, also read in one sitting and thoroughly enjoyable. Like before with the first novella, think of it as a rather gruesome version of *The X-Files*, with a nicely paced plot, engaging characters, humour and icky bits."

SFF World

"Another glorious gruesome ride with Ford and Neuland, everyone's favourite grim godfathers and Tilda, their more-than-able apprentice. Fast, furious and bloody. A novella with heart and other body parts."

A.G. Slatter

"With clever banter and cinematic style, the latest installation in Kadrey's *The Discreet Eliminators* series is a fun, satisfying, and refreshing noir romp!"

Kelsea Yu

"An expertly woven story of gruesome murders, eldritch magic, and dark streets flowing with blood... Kadrey puts flesh on the bones of a terrific tale, with prose reminiscent of Lansdale at his finest, and characters King would be proud of."

Tim Lebbon

"*The Flesh King* is like the second season of a great TV show. It deepens the world and expands the mythology. And most importantly, it gives us more of the twisty, turny, supernatural noir that we loved in *The Pale House Devil*. Bring on book 3!"

Shaun Hamill

Also by Richard Kadrey
and available from Titan Books

THE PALE HOUSE DEVIL